The turning place that the two young people took that day in the desert led them into unfamiliar terrain. And what they found down the strange canyon was the wall: invisible except for a bit of haziness, but nevertheless impenetrable—except in one place for a brief moment.

In the first of her nine stories, Jean Karl takes readers into the future and into a happening that is to change the whole nature of Earth's civilization. How the planet then evolves is the subject of the interrelated stories that follow—each very different, but each equally fascinating.

Born and raised in Chicago, JEAN E. KARL is a vice-president of Atheneum, a New York publishing house, and director of their children's book department, which she founded. She is the author of a book for adults, *From Childhood to Childhood: Children's Books and Their Creators.*

THE LAUREL-LEAF LIBRARY brings together under a single imprint outstanding works of fiction and nonfiction particularly suitable for young adult readers, both in and out of the classroom. The series is under the editorship of Charles F. Reasoner, Professor of Elementary Education, New York University.

THE TURNING PLACE

PLACE

STORIES OF
A FUTURE PAST

JEAN E. KARL

Published by
Dell Publishing Co., Inc.
1 Dag Hammarskjold Plaza
New York, New York 10017

Laurel-Leaf ® TM 766734, Dell Publishing Co., Inc.

ISBN: 0-440-98835-7

Reprinted by arrangement with E. P. Dutton & Co., Inc.
Printed in the United States of America
First Laurel-Leaf printing—November 1978

Most of all, for R. and W.

CONTENTS

THE TURNING PLACE

I don't know what to write. How much of what's happened should I put down? Where will I put this when I finish? Will anyone else ever see it? I can't be sure. I can't be sure of anything. That's one of the awful things. It's too hard to think about. There is nothing left to think about. No pattern. No matrix. Only the future. And the future is as blank as the desert below us.

It began four days ago. A morning like any other. At breakfast my father was reading his paper. He always did that. And my mother said, "Anything new in the paper? Anything cheerful for a change?" She almost always said that.

My father looked up and shook his head. "If anything it's worse."

"It can't be!"

"They can attack," said my father.

"But why?" my mother demanded. "Why?"

"I've explained," my father said. "Earth is too crowded. We need more room. A little more technical skill, and we can begin to plant some colonies in some nearby systems. But the Clordians don't want that to happen. They have this part of the galaxy sewn up. Or they thought they did until they discovered us."

"But surely there's enough space out there for all of us."

"Not enough within the technical limitations of either of us. It's a rotten shame that Clord is so close." He always said that. As if he were explaining again and again to himself. Trying to make sense of the whole senseless problem. "And worse still, they're so little ahead of us, just enough to be out there settling in while we've been feeling around here in the solar system. If only we'd moved a little faster. But, of course, we didn't know."

"Why didn't we? And why can't we do something? Work out an agreement of some sort? I don't understand why there can't be some reasonable way of settling this thing."

It was an old conversation in our house.

"I have nothing to do with that end of it. I don't know. I—well—some of our stuff may be useful in an attack; but we don't really have enough of anything to defend ourselves completely. And of course the Clordians know that."

My father is, or was, a particle physicist. We lived in a town on the desert, with mountains all around. It was nice. There were houses and green grass and stores and schools and the laboratory. The laboratory was where most of the fathers and mothers worked. It was a big place, run by the government mostly, although some private industries contributed. Everyone in the lab was working on atoms, not atoms really, but mesons and quarks and all that. Basic energy, my father called it. "Nothing," I used to tell him, "you're dealing with nothing." Because that's what it seemed like to me.

But that was four days ago. And that morning I didn't worry too much about the Clordians. We discovered them (or they discovered us, however you want to look at it) fifteen years ago, and I was only born thirteen years ago, so the problem's always been there for me. As my father said, it was tough that they were so near us in the galaxy and so little ahead of us technically. Far enough ahead, and we wouldn't have been in their way. Behind us, and we would have been their problem. As it was, it's been one threat after another. We hardly even dared go to the moon. We could have just given up, I guess, but nobody wanted to. Not that they wanted to conquer us. They don't need this planet. They just didn't want us out here competing with them while they moved colonies into the planets they did want. They saw that we too were crowded, even with all our population-control laws. And they didn't trust us.

Yet, four days ago the Clordians didn't seem any bigger a problem than usual, and I ignored them. As soon as I could, I dealt with something more important.

"Can I go out on the desert with Krishna today?" He lived next door. His father was part of the international team at the lab. Krishna and I both liked the desert. Every once in a while we hiked out there together. No one else we knew liked to go.

"Well, I don't know, Georgia . . ." My mother didn't like the desert much. She was a people lover, the town pediatrician. There were times when I felt as if all the kids I knew were related to me. She was proxy mother to all of them.

"Oh, why not," said my father, who didn't understand about the desert either, but who kept feeling I was being overprotected. "It's December. It won't be too hot. Christmas vacation is the ideal time to go to the desert, if you have to go."

My mother gave in. She always did. So Krishna and I set out about half an hour later. We each had a compass, a knapsack with plenty of water, some food, the usual first-aid stuff, and a communicator.

When we walked in the desert, we almost always went the same way. In fact, our parents had laid down rules about desert-walking. They weren't too rigid, so we really tried to keep them. We stayed on established trails. We never walked more than three or four hours out. We wore hats and all the usual desert gear. And we took along a small communicator in case we got lost or in trouble, although neither of us would have wanted to use it. We both felt we'd have to be pretty stupid to get into the kind of fix where we'd need it. After all, we were never very far from civilization, and we almost always ran into at least one person, out walking or riding.

There was only one trail up into the desert. It started at the north edge of town, led up a smallish hill, then down and up into the mountains. After a while it branched off. There were at least ten branches that we knew of. Krishna and I had explored most of them. Some led to abandoned mines, others to tumbledown shacks, and some went on over the mountains to places beyond our four-hour range.

There was one branch, though, that we hadn't followed. It turned off about two kilometers down the main trail. And, though we couldn't understand why, we had noticed it for the first time just a couple of weeks ago. We'd been that far at least a dozen times before, but we hadn't seen the path. And we felt we ought to check it out. At least I felt that way. Krishna didn't care as long as he was in the desert.

So four days ago, we started down this new trail. It surprised us. It curved around, out of sight of the main path, and almost immediately it took us into really strange country. There were more rocks, loose rocks, along the way than usual. And the path, narrow at the start, got even narrower. We had to walk single file, and sometimes we were pressed close against the sharp rocks of a canyon wall.

The path led at first up a fairly wide canyon, where the walls beside us were not too steep. After about a half hour, however, we turned into a much narrower canyon, almost a gorge.

We moved steadily up a path on our side of the canyon. On the other side, another path moved up also. Both lay some distance above the canyon floor, but I felt from the look of things that the two paths, and perhaps the canyon floor also, would meet at the head of the canyon. I couldn't tell for sure because there were slight twists to the canyon itself that made it impossible to see that far ahead.

As we moved forward the canyon sides above us gradually became more sloping. We rounded a curve, and then suddenly I stopped. The end of the canyon was about five hundred meters ahead. But I couldn't go on. I had come to something that blocked me. It was a wall that didn't look like a wall. In fact, it was a wall I couldn't see at all. There was a bit of haziness, no more. Yet I couldn't move through it.

"See if you can feel this, too," I said to Krishna, who had stopped to look at a rock, and now came strolling up.

Without saying anything, he came up next to me. We squeezed together on the path, and he put his hands ahead.

"What do you make of it?" I asked.

He didn't answer. Instead he felt along the wall. It curved out over the drop across to the other side of the canyon. At least it went as far as we could reach. It also went up the slope beside us. We could see through it, and yet it blocked our way.

Without words, acting almost instinctively, we pulled ourselves up and climbed above the path. We followed the wall far enough to see that it curved on and on—probably right around the mountain at the canyon head. Then we hurried back to the path. I think we both wanted to be on something that felt familiar.

As far as we could see, the head of the canyon was perfectly ordinary. It had a shallow cave, or the entrance to an old mine, at the end, just above the path. The path did curve around just above the slanting floor of the canyon, as I had thought it would.

"Maybe the men from the lab are doing something here," I said. "That could explain why we didn't see the path before. It could be new. This wall could be some kind of force field."

"No," said Krishna, "no. It isn't that. There'd be NO TRESPASSING signs. And besides, there's no machinery."

"It could be projected from something below. Even from town," I said.

"No," said another voice, a strange voice from behind me, a man. Krishna and I hadn't heard anyone coming, and the voice frightened us. "You could be right, but you're not," it went on.

I turned nervously to look at the man. We both did, both more upset than we normally would have been because we were still puzzled by the wall. The stranger didn't seem to be a monster or a man from some planet of Alpha Centauri. He was a plain man, in everyday hiking clothes, with a pack and a walking stick.

"Don't worry," he said. "I'm not dangerous. And I'm not sure this is a danger. But it's something to check out. They've been aware of it for several days at the Central Energy Bank. And I'm the one who's supposed to decide what it is. More to the point, I'm the only one who was willing to climb out here."

"What do you think it is?" I asked, louder than I meant to.

"I'm not sure," he said again. "It's not a normal force field. I know that. And it's not from the lab in your town. It's different from anything they could make there."

"Then where's it from?" I asked.

"I haven't seen enough to know," he said. "I'm an electrical engineer, and I've done a lot of work with the new uses of nuclear binding forces. But I've never seen anything quite like this—not so big and strong, and yet so neutral. It made a lot of static over at the lab. Even so, I didn't expect something so solid."

"Which lab?" I said. "If not ours."

"The one over at Clistra. The unified field project."

He grinned and rubbed his chin. "I was down at your place seeing some people to get their ideas. And then came up here. I'm mostly Indian. American Indian," he added, looking at Krishna. "My ancestors roamed these mountains, so they always seem like home, even though I've never lived in them. I was glad for a chance to get up here. But now I'm not so sure this is where I want to be."

"You didn't make the path?" I asked. It seemed a foolish question, but the path was puzzling me too. Why hadn't we seen it before? Did it have something to do with the wall?

He shrugged. "No. But you're right, it could be quite new; the edges are sharp." I hadn't had sense enough to realize that.

He turned and felt the wall again, then reached into his pack and took out some small instruments. We watched him as he poked and prodded. After a bit, he took out some other gear and did more quick tests. When he turned to us again, his face was tense.

"This is not created by anything on Earth," he said positively.

"From where, then?" I whispered.

"From Clord?" Krishna murmured.

The man rubbed his chin and nodded. "Maybe."

"We'd better go," I said, getting my voice back. "We'd better tell somebody."

"Look," he said, "stay a while. I may need you. I've got to do some more checking. I want to be sure before I report anything. And I may need some help."

He ran through his tests again, very intensely. When

he finished, he turned to us, obviously baffled. "It's a field, of some sort. But what kind, and what for?"

"Do you want me to use my communicator?" I asked.

He shook his head. "Too dangerous so close," he said. "The wrong ones might hear. In fact, I think walking down to your place would be the best way to report. The safest."

That really threw me.

"He's right," Krishna said slowly. "We've got to be careful. My father has been worried. . . ." He drifted off. "For now we should stay here—learn all we can. Then we should go down."

I was outvoted. Well, not really. I had nothing to cast my vote for except going home. And suddenly I didn't want that either. There seemed to be more to do where we were. Maybe it was wrong, but we stayed.

For a few minutes we just stood there, thinking. Then without a word we all put our hands on the wall and pushed. Nothing happened.

"Maybe it takes a fourth, like a bridge." This time there were three of us to be startled by a strange voice. It belonged to a woman in riding clothes.

"Why, there is a wall here," she said, reaching out, as if she thought we'd all been pushing on air. "Whatever is it?"

We told her what we knew.

"Is there a break in it anywhere?" she asked.

"Not that we've found," the man answered.

"We went way up," I said. "And we couldn't find a break."

"We might know more about it if we could get inside," the man said. "Let's see what we can do."

So all four of us trooped up the way Krishna and I had gone, but this time we went farther up along the wall. Krishna was first, and all at once he gave a little cry.

"It's here," he said. "The entrance."

Sure enough, there was a break of about a meter, as if two huge plates of steel hung for a wall didn't quite meet at the joining. The woman pushed on through, and hardly thinking, we all walked in behind.

Inside was much like outside, the same rock, the same contours. There was a little more vegetation, but that was normal since we had reached the more shaded areas at the head of the canyon. I felt along the curve. The wall was as firm on one side as on the other. We explored around, then climbed down to the path inside the wall and marched to the head of the canyon. There was no sign of anyone or anything. We stood there, looking from side to side, surrounded by a strange translucent haze.

"Nothing more here," said the man reluctantly.

"Not even my runaway horse," said the woman, ruefully. "I thought he might be up here. Got spooked by a snake when I got off to look at a new rockfall. I thought he came this way."

None of us had seen a horse.

"Well, let's go back," said the man. "No more to find here. We might as well report what we can."

We went back to the break in the wall. We had marked the way with cairns, and left a special pile of rocks just at the hole. But the hole wasn't there. We felt around the wall, slowly at first, then with a frantic desperation. There was no hole. The opening was gone.

I got mad then. I had been curious, like the rest. But not curious enough to get caught in a trap. "Get us out," I shouted at the woman. "We have to go home. Our parents will worry. You led us in here. Now get us out."

The woman looked upset herself. "I just didn't think," she said. "I was so intent on finding my horse. I'm Leslie Frame. I have a ranch about ten miles away—down near Corba. I ride up this way often, especially at this time of year, and I suppose I've been in this canyon a dozen times. It never occurred to me to be afraid. I just wasn't thinking."

"It was my fault," said the man, looking at me. "I should have known better. I didn't want to admit the truth. And now we're trapped."

"But what is it?" Leslie asked. "What is the wall?"

"A field of some sort," the man said. "Clordian, I suspect. Not dangerous now, but it could be. Though how they intend to use it, I don't know."

"Where from?" Krishna asked.

"A spaceship of some sort, I would judge—maybe even a space platform. If it's high enough, we wouldn't catch it. Not with the kind of diffusion screen they're likely to use. By the way, I'm Victor Tallhill."

"I'm Georgia West, and this is Krishna Raspinti."

"Can we get out?" Krishna asked.

"We can try," Victor said. "There may be another break. But I rather doubt it. If this one is closed, any others are probably closed too."

We moved along the wall, staying together. But there was no break, not even a place where the wall didn't quite touch the ground. We were well out of sight of the path when Victor stopped us.

"If we haven't found a break by now," he said, "we won't find one. After all, this wall is not here by accident. What is sealed, is sealed. Let's stop and see what we do know. The wall is a field, neutral now, probably projected by equipment shielded from our protective warning systems. If I read the field right, it can be used to transmit a lot of things. It may also be able to move, to enlarge. If the transmitter is strong enough, and the thing can move, it may be able to sweep a large area. If it's Clordian, it must be a new thing. They haven't had this before. We'd have known. They've been working very quietly." His face was very drawn now. And all of us sensed why. This was a threat, a danger bigger than we had thought before.

I felt as if I couldn't breathe. We were all quiet—too long. I had to say something.

"Can't we warn somebody? The communicator. . . ."

"Will never penetrate the wall," said Victor.

"You can't be sure," I said.

"Of that much I can be sure," he answered. "But the strange thing is—the really terrible part for us—is that we may be safe."

"Safe?" murmured Leslie.

"If it moves out, we may not be touched by what it carries. It all depends, of course, on what they plan."

I had to think a minute about that. And then I realized why that was so terrible. I beat against the wall then, and Krishna kicked at it. But it did no good. We were inside to stay.

"Can't we warn anyone?" Krishna asked at last.

"What good would it do?" Victor asked. "We

couldn't get even all the people in your town inside this circle. And, of course, we don't know for sure that we'll be safe here. We don't even know what's going to happen. Maybe it's nothing. Or maybe it's better for people not to know. I think that whatever happens will come soon. A field of this size can be detected and checked. It won't stand idle long."

"What about our parents?" I said. "Will they die?"

"Depends on what the plans for this are," he said.

"Will it be only here—or everywhere?" Krishna asked.

I looked at him, startled. "What difference does it make?" I asked. "If our parents are gone, what will we do?"

"Don't panic. It won't help," Krishna said, as if he hadn't been close to panic too, a moment before. "There are many ways of living. In spite of entropy, my father says, nothing is ever really lost."

Krishna is my age. But sometimes he seems too old. How could he be so abstract when everyone we knew was in danger?

"But our parents!" I shouted at him. "Our parents may die!"

His face crumpled, and I was immediately sorry. He was only trying to help.

"We don't know for sure," Victor said softly. "We are here by chance, maybe, and we have to do the best we can, until we see what happens."

Leslie Frame looked thoughtful. "If that's true, then we'd better start working. The nights are cold up here in December."

"There was a cave or an old mine or something at the head of the canyon," I said dully. I had to pull myself together. I couldn't keep making things worse for us. After all, as Victor said, we didn't really know anything.

We made our way back to the path, then moved to the head of the canyon again. It was an old mine. Most of it had fallen in, but there was enough that seemed safe at the front to shelter us. There were even some old timbers around, evidently intended for the mine and never used. They would make fine firewood.

We had begun to check our resources when we heard voices coming up the path. We were startled, then hopeful. Was the wall gone? Had someone found a way through?

We raced out of the mine and saw a group of people coming toward us, not from our path, but the path on the other side of the canyon. There were four kids and two adults, who seemed to be together. Behind them were two men who seemed separate. The family looked frightened; the men looked puzzled.

In a few minutes we met. One of the men spoke first.

"What in blazes is this? Do you know? I never saw anything like it!"

Victor and Leslie explained as best they could. It took a long time for the new people to understand. It helped me, in a way, to hear it all said once again. It made it more real, and at the same time, more unreal, if that makes sense.

When the talking was finished, the men sat on the ground, and so did the kids. The other adults were leaning against the entrance to the mine. We knew what they were thinking. The men probably had wives and kids outside. A couple of the kids maybe had other parents. Four was too many for one family. We felt sorry for them—and us.

"I'm Georgia West," I said finally, to break the awful silence. I introduced the other three in our group. Then the others gave their names. The men were John Biggs and Gray Skopotkin, mining engineers. They'd flown in by helicopter at dawn to look for an old mine, supposed to be in the area somewhere, that they thought would yield up some Rare Earths. They'd come through a haze, but not a wall, searched the other side of the mountain, then found that the haze had hardened and they couldn't get through. The wall ringed the whole upper part of the mountain as far as they could tell.

"And this may be your mine," I said.

They nodded grimly.

The family was Peter and Susan De Fleshe, and Betsy (10), Tony (7), Jill (11), and Tom (8). Only Jill and Tom were De Fleshes. Betsy and Tony were cousins, on their way to visit their grandparents for a couple of weeks. The six of them had seen a strange haze from their air car and stopped to check it out, just for a lark. Like us, they had come through a crack and been trapped. They hadn't even planned to come this way. Just taken a new route for a change.

Now here we all were. We looked at each other, then went into the mine to finish what the four of us had begun, only now there were twelve of us. We went to work in silence, getting a fire ready, checking on the space available, and wondering how long we would have to wait, what would happen before we could leave. No one spoke, except the little kids, and even they were quiet, as if they sensed the dreadful chasm that lay before the rest of us.

"What about food?" asked Susan.

"We four had started a pool," said Leslie. "I didn't have much with me. I was chasing a runaway horse. But I always carry a few things when I go into the desert. Victor and Georgia and Krishna had quite a bit."

"We've got some," said John Biggs, quietly. "We'd planned to camp. We left our gear over the ridge a way. I think maybe we'd better get it."

The two men left, plodding along heavily, yet moving swiftly. Like the rest of us, they seemed to be moving in a purposeful dream, a dream we would wake up from and know had been a nightmare.

"Let's go over to the wall again," I said to Krishna. I wanted to be sure, really sure, that we were trapped before I finally gave in.

Nothing had changed. The wall was there. If anything, it was a bit more obvious, and a bit thicker. You could see through, but not as much.

"It's heavier," I said to Krishna.

He nodded, and we walked back to the mine.

Victor was outside, and the mining engineers came soon after, with their gear. They dumped it, and we all stood watching, looking at the wall. It was growing visibly thicker, even from a distance.

"Back into the mine entrance," Victor said finally. "We might as well be as safe as we can."

We moved, but not all the way in. Something was happening, and we had to watch.

Five minutes passed—maybe—or five hours. We stared as if our eyes were tied to the distance ahead.

Eventually the wall grew green. Then flashes of yellow sparked through it. And slowly it began to move out. At first it was almost as if one man was trying to push a heavy truck over the top of the hill. The wall didn't want to go. But then its pace quickened as if the top of the hill had been reached and the weight was being pushed along a plane.

By the time it really started to move, everyone was watching, even the little kids, who didn't know at all what was happening. Of course, none of us did either, not for sure.

"There she goes," called Tony. But his tone was subdued.

The huge flickering green and yellow cylinder, or what we could see of it, began spreading faster. It moved quietly for a bit, drawing away, then suddenly *whooshed* out with a roar that deafened us and left us weak with fright and wonder. It was gone before we knew.

"Can it go all around the Earth?" Krishna asked.

Victor and the miners nodded. "This one, or maybe a bunch of them," one said.

I hadn't thought of that. More than one. Were there others trapped as we were, then, in the middle of a circle?

Finally we all went into the mine entrance. We had watched, and now we couldn't stand to watch anymore. It was better not to see. Not to think.

"Now that it's gone, can we go?" Jill asked.

She still didn't understand. So Victor explained what we were afraid had happened. Jill's mouth dropped. The two boys began to cry. I felt like it. And so did all the others, I guess. We all just sat still, unable to move, unable to lift the terrible burden of what we believed.

"We have to plan," said Victor, finally, trying once again to get us into motion—to save us from our thoughts. "For now, we must stay here. Tomorrow, maybe the day after, we'll move down a bit. But not before. Maybe someone will miss us and come looking. Then we'll know it's safe."

"Can we check the food?" said Susan De Fleshe, weakly, looking up from Tony, who now sat on her lap.

It turned out that when it was all pooled, there was quite a bit of food. The two miners had planned to stay several days. While I was checking to make sure all of mine was in the pool, I came upon my communicator. I held it out wordlessly.

Leslie shook her head, but Victor took it. "Might work now," he said. Somehow, he had become a sort of leader, although what little we were doing was largely by common consent. We were doing the best we could. But we were all slow, drugged by terror and horror. We didn't know what was happening, what to think.

Victor turned on my communicator. "The band?" he asked. I told him. He tried, and there was nothing. But that was the closest place. He tried some others that he knew. Nothing there either. "A hundred-mile range at most. And the field may still be in the way," he said.

It was no comfort.

We made our arrangements then. The mine wasn't very big, not room enough in the safe part for twelve. And only the mining engineers had sleeping bags. It would be cold at night, but even so, I decided I would prefer the outside. Finally it was decided that the two women and the two young boys would stay inside. The rest of us would find places on the mountain. There were flat places, and we could gather some brush for mattresses and blankets.

"Just stay away from snake holes," said Victor. Somehow snakes didn't seem such a menace just then. We even made some arrangements for sanitation facilities. Victor was very thorough. He kept us busy, and at the same time kept himself busy too. It was the only way to keep your mind from groping at the future.

Water was going to be our next problem. We had enough for the night. But after that we'd need more. Tomorrow would be time enough to search, Victor decided. For water and whatever else we might try to find.

That night out in the open was strange. The sky wasn't right, but none of us knew what was wrong. Something was still happening in the atmosphere. But what it was we did not know, and did not even want to imagine. None of us slept much. John Biggs and Gray Skopotkin paced a small piece of mountain most of the night, never speaking, just pacing, until, almost at the same moment, they both dropped into their sleeping bags, worn out. I envied them in a way and wished I had done the same—exercise until I dropped. Krishna had stayed near the mine, and he said later that the women talked quietly most of the night. Only the two little boys really slept.

Morning was clear. It almost always is in this part of the country. But the horizon was too near, and dusty. It was hard to tell why. We knew about the moving field, of course. But it was gone. What was the dust?

After breakfast, tired as we all were, we felt that we had to do something. Do anything. So we divided up and set out in different directions. We were to stay pretty much inside the area the field had once enclosed. Krishna and Victor and I were to climb to the top of the mountain, the rise above the mine. The others, in three groups, were going to follow the path both ways and also explore the canyon floor below the mine. Water was our main need, the spoken object of our search. But all of us knew that everyone would be looking for some sign of what might lie in the world beyond.

We all three picked our way up the hill. Five hundred meters is a long way up, stumbling back and forth across a mountain, even when it is not too steep. We didn't say much. At the top we slumped down and took a small sip of water from the canteen we shared. Then we looked out to see what was there. It had never been a place where you could see people. That was clear. But we didn't like the haze that still muddied the distance. Something had been stirred up that wasn't yet ready to settle. And there were fewer green spots than we might have expected. But we'd never, any of us, seen the view from up there before. We couldn't say it looked different.

"Better stay in the canyon until it's clear," Victor said.

We just nodded. It sounded good. We weren't eager to go down. Unless someone came up for us.

We picked our way back to the mine, looking for

water and maybe something edible. Not much luck. The others had been a little more successful, especially the ones who went down the canyon floor—Leslie Frame, Jill, and Tom. Leslie had found water. There had been some edible greens down there too. Jill and Tom each had a handful. John Biggs, who had wandered off the path onto the hill with Peter De Fleshe, had shot a rabbit with the small rifle he carried. The others, like us, had found nothing. We sat just looking into the distance then, not seeing anything. Most of the rest of the day we were still, except for a water-carrying, green-gathering expedition in the middle of the afternoon. The frantic activity of yesterday no longer seemed an answer to our worry. Some of us slept finally. But none of us slept all through the night when it came. I kept seeing my parents, wondering. . . .

The next day the haze began to settle. And surprisingly there was rain. Not the torrential rain of the desert, but a gentle rain that came and stayed a while. I wondered if the whole world was raining. We caught what we could, and Victor and Gray tested it with their equipment. It seemed safe, and we drank it.

The rain stopped before night, and the ground was not too wet for sleeping. Rain disappears quickly in the desert.

"We'll go down tomorrow," Victor said. "Slowly. Testing our way. Not taking chances. We could live here a while longer but we need to move out, I think. We need to know more. We can't just sit. We have to keep going."

"Why not take chances," said John Biggs, almost laughing. "What have we got to lose?"

"It's not what *we* have to lose," said Victor. "It's what the world has to lose."

No one said anything more. We all understood. But no one could say it. What if everyone were dead? Could we stand it? How would we act? We drew together, needing each other and all the bravery each of us had to give. A group. That's what we had to be. Not individuals, but all one. Yet inside we were still separate from each other. We each had our own hopes and our own griefs. We were afraid alone. We could not share our fears because we each hoped privately that we would not have to face them. As a group we knew better, and we needed each other in order to do what we had to do, in order to go on.

Finally Victor told us an old Indian tale—one about the world being destroyed three times, and each time new life emerging better than before. The story made too much sense, and no sense at all. Betsy was the only one who cried. The rest of us were too old or too young.

We went to bed under clear skies and the stars we have always known. There was nothing strange left up there. Yet none of us was sure, I think, if the sky was a good place or just a place of death.

It is morning now. I started this yesterday because the others said I must. I did it while we waited out the rain in the mine, and later, by the campfire. Leslie Frame had a pad of paper in her knapsack. I've written before. For the school paper. But I didn't want to do this. I had to, they said.

We are going down. At least we are going to start down. We will go the way Krishna and I came up, down to our town. If we find what we expect, Krishna and I will meet our sorrow first. But in what form, we do not know.

"If the worst is what we find," said John Biggs this morning, "then we've got to stick together. We aren't a family. There's no love between us. Yet apart we can't survive. And we must survive." He seemed grim but determined. Better than yesterday. We are all learning to consider only the moment as individuals. To plan for the future as a whole. Then he added, "We will not be all alone, surely. There have to be others, somewhere. We may find them, and we may not. We may have no way of finding them. Either way, those left are Victor's new emergence. For whatever it means."

We stood silent a moment. And Victor threw up his hand and looked at the sky.

No one cried this morning. It is too late for that here. But below, who knows?

We may be stronger than I think. It may be chance that brought us together, and it may not be. Yet I believe we must try to live; we must try to flourish together, alone in the world, if need be.

This story is for us; for anyone we may find; and for those who must come after us. It goes down the mountain with us.

OVER THE HILL

Carpa paused to catch her breath. Tired, and it was barely past dawn. She wished she had slept better these nights in the open. It would make the long, trudging days easier. Yet she would not stop. She would not give in. She would find a place. Wearily she lifted her feet. Better to get as far as she could before the sun got too high and the heat made motion more difficult. It was warm already. Good growing weather. She made a face to herself. What difference did it make? Yet it did matter—it mattered for the place she would find. But where was it? How far? If she could find a resting place only for a day, it would help. The chance of finding a home or even a spot where she would be welcomed for more than a few hours seemed unlikely now. It had been five days—or was it six? Yet—surely soon—there would at least be people somewhere.

Why had her mother, her father, even, seemed to think it would not be hard? Because she was strong and determined? Maybe. But maybe too, because that's what they had wanted to think. She had had to leave. They knew it and so had put the best face on it. They would never know what happened. Could always think the best. Only she would know for sure. And she had to make it! She was going to make it!

She sighed again. Curse the land! The endless, barren, hard land, with its only occasional lush valleys. Growing space for so little. Each valley a place for so few. Her parents, her grandparents too, were all alive, and there was her brother. Their land had been enough for six. But when the woman came over the hill and her brother wanted her to stay, to become his wife, someone had had to go. There would be children, maybe more than the two she and her brother had been. Their land was not enough.

Sometimes, she had heard her grandmother say, it was a man who left when a growing place grew too crowded. But more often it was a woman. She wandered until she found a place where she was wanted, or until her food gave out. Whichever came first.

Her food supply was low, but not too low. She had been careful. And in one or two places she had found plants. That had surprised her. You didn't expect to see plants growing just anywhere. These had been near a stream. Washed down, maybe. But still, growing in the dead earth. And good to eat.

With a tug she pulled herself to the top of the rise. Up another obstacle. Another climb behind her. Down would be easier. Not looking up—after all, one dead valley was like another—she put one foot in front of the other, easing herself down the casual grade.

Water. She could use water. Glancing up then, she hoped to see water ahead. The last valley had been dry. She looked and then focused her gaze sharply. It was hard to believe. She was seeing things because she'd been alone so long! But no, there was water, and more. Stopping, she stared in wonder. This was a growing valley! Crops high and lush. A house and small planted fields. Oats, corn, vegetables. All the things she knew. Even some trees. Her brother's wife had told of them. But there were none in Carpa's home valley. Was it possible? After all this time!

She moved cautiously down. There was no way of knowing who lived here. How many people. They might be welcoming. They might not. No one was to be seen. Yet she had to be careful. They'd have no cause to hurt her. Still, it was best to be cautious.

She moved into the corn. It rose high on either side, but not high enough to hide her. She half bent down, covering herself; wanting time to observe, to see who was here to decide what to do.

It was too late. She had been seen. A boy, her own age she guessed, was coming. He strode toward her, then bent to pick up a stick. Why that? What was he afraid of? What was the matter?

She stood up quickly, wanting the advantage of her full height. She stepped out, moving to meet him, head held high. He should see she came honestly, not to steal. The stick rose menacingly in his hand, then dropped. Had he decided she wasn't dangerous?

He spoke. The words were clear. They almost made sense, and yet they didn't. Her brother's wife had been the same—yet her words had been more like theirs, Carpa felt.

She replied, speaking the words of morning greeting carefully. But she could see he didn't understand. She smiled, pointed to her knapsack, then to the hill from which she had come. He nodded gravely, but looked upset again. Was it possible no wanderer had ever come to this valley in his lifetime?

Motioning to her to follow, he led the way toward the house. She wondered if she should go. With the boy so unsettled, would there be trouble at the house? Yet she needed water. And maybe there would be food and a chance to rest. Even a little food would make what she carried last longer. And a day of rest would give the strength she had to have.

They came to the house, and he pointed to a bench outside. She was to sit there. She did so gratefully. It was a nice place. A good house—fine stones. A good garden too, but in need of some weeding and picking. That was easily done. And the trees! Two stood behind the bench, reaching up, with leaves, and roundish green fruit of some sort. Almost yellow, those at the top.

She glanced back at the boy and smiled again. He looked puzzled. Then he smiled, just a little himself. Why didn't he get the others, she wondered. She pointed at the house and nodded. Best to get it over with.

He didn't understand. He glanced at the house, then at her. Motioning her to be still, he disappeared inside. In a few moments he was out with some meat. Rabbit. And some raw carrots. She ate hungrily. She hadn't realized how dull her diet had become. The boy just stood and stared at her. Then when she had finished all he had given her, he came and stood on the bench and reached high up, up to the yellow fruit at the top. She held her breath. Was she to taste it? It was more than she had hoped for. If only no one came to stop him. Maybe that's what worried him.

He handed her the fruit. She smiled, grinned really, at him. It was all she could do in thanks. Then she bit into the fruit. It was soft and sweet and juicy. The juice ran down her chin and she reached down as far as she could with her tongue. Swept the rest up with her finger and into her mouth. It was too good to lose any. Again the boy just stood and stared.

She glanced around once more as she swallowed the last of the fruit. Where were the others? She looked at the vegetables. Surely someone should be weeding. She got up and stepped over to the beans, pulled a weed. Maybe he would let her weed a little in payment for food. The boy looked at her in alarm again. Picked up the stick he had dropped.

That was no good. What next? He looked desperate now. As if he didn't know which way to turn. Maybe she should leave. She reached for her bag. But he stopped her. Put out his hand. Then he made a sweeping, reaping motion. He pointed to the oats. Maybe that's where the others were. But she saw no one. The oats did need harvesting. It was almost past time. With another gesture that seemed to indicate she should say, he disappeared toward the oats. In a few minutes she saw him cutting away at it, alone.

What did it mean? What was she to do? Stay as long as she was welcome, obviously. And show that she could be useful. Maybe that would at least earn a night's rest. And a bit more of that fruit.

With a practiced hand she moved down a row of beans. First she drew out the weeds. They robbed the soil, her father had said. Then she picked the beans that were ready. From one row she went to the next. And from beans to peas and squash. It was a good garden, in spite of the weeds. But under her care, it could be even better. She thought with satisfaction of the garden she had left behind. It had been hers alone for the past two summers. It wasn't fair to have to leave! She sighed. It couldn't be helped.

The quiet oppressed her again. There was something wrong here. Why was she picking someone else's beans and peas and squash, weeding them, when she had seen only the boy? Better to leave before something happened.

She rose suddenly, her back tired. She had been weary before she began. Would there really be a place for her, somewhere? Or would her food give out first? Better not to think of that! She looked ruefully at the beans she had gathered, the peas. All in a safe little pile. Better leave them. No sense in calling down trouble. At least she'd paid for what she'd eaten.

The boy was coming, whistling. A lot more cheerful than he had been. What now? He waved. Too late to leave before he came.

The boy looked in surprise at the vegetables she had picked, put on the bench, and at the weeded rows. Did he think she was ignorant? He smiled then, more than before, and beckoned toward the house. Should she go in? What kind of trap could it be? She hesitated. Then decided to take a chance. She had so little to lose.

Hesitantly she followed the boy in. It was pleasant, well furnished. Spare but comfortable. She looked around with pleasure. Would there be some other such house to receive her somewhere?

The boy went to the fire, still burning from the morning, took up some pots, and went to a cupboard.

Dried meat, vegetables, all in the pot. And some water. But was there no one else?

For the first time it struck her that the boy might be alone. But how could that be? He should have parents, grandparents, maybe even a brother or a sister. She looked around again. But there was no one.

The boy stood up and looked at her. She saw that he knew what she was thinking, and a flash of fear crossed his face. Of course. That was the answer. He was alone. Everyone dead or gone for some reason. No wonder he acted so oddly. She was a stranger, and he was alone. She remembered how her father had warned of the dangers a stranger might bring. Yet there had been only three or four who had come in all the years she could remember, and none of them had ever been dangerous. There weren't many people to come, she knew that now. This boy was the first person she had seen since she left her own valley. Yet her family had been afraid. Was it because they didn't know? Her mother had come over the hill, though she said little of it. Maybe not from so far. This boy, she knew, had never been away. He couldn't know. Maybe, too, no one had ever told him how girls sometimes came over the hills. Could she tell him? Was there any way to say it that wouldn't frighten him? There was certainly room here if he would let her stay.

She smiled at the boy, to reassure him. And she made herself as useful as she could without being too forward. Before long they were eating together. Then the boy tried again at conversation. She could see that the words were not unlike. Some she almost recognized. And with signs she made him understand that she had come from far, that she was seeking a new home. She conveyed her approval of his house, his fields. And she saw pride mingle with unease and fear, still. Fear was greater when you felt alone and vulnerable. She was alone too, and knew. Yet to try to say this would only frighten him more.

The meal ended in an unsettled haze. Should she stay or should she go? It would mean so much to stay in a comfortable place, if only for one night. If she could just sleep before she went on, that would be something. For a moment she had the stark notion of overcoming the boy, driving him off. Stupid. She couldn't, and she really didn't want to. Then she would always have to be afraid of the same thing herself: if she knew for sure people did that, because she had done it herself, she could not rest easy.

They left the house together after the meal-cleaning was done. He motioned to the bench and said a few words. Was she to stay? It seemed so. But she saw that he was agitated. She knew how the pattern of life went on a farm, the pressures he was under, alone at this season. No wonder the weeding wasn't done. There was too much work for one. And if he were newly alone, he might wonder, as she did, if he could cope with the future.

Did she want to stay here with this boy? For more than a day? The question made her stop. He was such a stolid sort. A child almost, though surely of her age. At ease with her himself, he might be different. Yet it was nothing for her to ponder now. It was his land and his decision. If he wanted her to stay, then it would be her turn to decide. She could stay or she could go. She was no beggar to remain in a sorry place, just to live.

She turned again to the garden to keep from thinking. Warring against her sensible thoughts, her pride, was a feeling of desperation. She had to find a place, and soon. This was the first in five—or was it six—days. Could she manage to get to another? And would she be welcome there if she found it? These were not the thoughts she wanted. She tried to put them away, but they kept coming back.

The afternoon wore on. The boy, when she looked, was not in the oats. Where had he gone? She gathered up what she had picked and put them with the ones from the morning, on the bench. Enough here to dry, she thought absently.

The futility of it struck her. What chance did she have? How could she survive another six days, let alone winter, if she didn't find a place? And this boy! It was clear he was too confused, too unsettled, to let her stay long. She dropped her head, willing herself not to cry. And as she did, he came up. She looked at him and knew. She had been right. She was to go.

What had happened? Agitated, he motioned for her to be gone, to pick up her bag and go. Fear had won over his obvious need for companionship. Well, so be it. She couldn't say what she thought because he wouldn't understand. She seized what was hers and set off. Head high again, she almost ran. She wouldn't even look back. What was there here for her? Her future lay beyond.

Halfway to the hill ahead, she felt an urgent tap on her arm. The boy. Had he changed his mind? Was he calling her back? No, some vegetables. For her bag.

He motioned for her to open it. That was thoughtful, at least. She opened the bag, and he put them in; but she didn't look at him. Couldn't bear to let him see her disappointment. And her anger. Suddenly she blazed with fury. He had everything, and she had nothing. And he shared a few vegetables! What did he think she was? Well, she didn't need him. She'd find her own place, her own way. And so much for the likes of him.

"All right," she said, still not looking at him. "You choose to live alone. I cannot help you then. Even in a few days I could have done a lot for that neglected garden. But the choice is yours, and you made it. I wish you well of it."

She looked at him, determined and grim, and he seemed bewildered. She had no intention of smiling, yet she did; because, she saw, his need was almost as great as hers, though he didn't know it. Then she hurried off. Let him think what he would.

She moved quickly toward the hill and up. Anger and determination alike surged through her, made her strong. But as she climbed, the old weariness overcame her and she moved more slowly, less positively. Still, she did not look back. And she kept moving.

It was late afternoon when she reached the hilltop. A lovely time of day. She yearned to stop, to rest there. And maybe she would. Yet she needed water; she'd fortotten to get it; or rather, she had hardly been given time or opportunity. Water would more likely lie below than on the hilltop.

She sank to the ground for a rest and became aware for the first time that she had not been traveling over dry, hard dirt. There were bits of lichen and mosses, and in many places, where the dirt was loosened, scatterings of other plants as well. Some of them she recognized as edible. Up here! Not close along a stream! What did it mean? Always the land had been dry and hard, except in the scattered places, in the protected valleys, where all things grew. Did this mean that all land might now grow things, if it were dug up and planted? If that was true, she need never have left home. She could go back.

The idea was curiously unappealing. Her leave-taking had been too final. And her journey had changed her. She could not go home and be the person she had been. She didn't want to be the child in the family anymore. She could only go on.

Rising, she moved to the edge of the hill and looked down. What she saw took her breath away. Made her momentarily afraid. A city of the old ones! She had heard of such. One who had come through their valley had said that there were places where many had once lived. Though how, no one understood. And here was such a place. She had never been sure she could believe in them before. But it was true.

She seized her sack and hurried on. Was this the answer? If there was growth here too, could she not live here alone? These dwellings must surely still provide some shelter. She could harvest the things she knew, range far and wide if need be, kill rabbits. They must like such old warrens as these houses were. The idea gave her feet wings. She all but ran down the hill to arrive before the twilight was upon her.

Once at the bottom of the hill, she moved more slowly. Best to be sure no one was there. Though the place looked deserted.

She moved cautiously into the ruins, amazed. There must have been a hundred houses here once. Some seemed to have been of wood, but almost none of the wood was left. Only a hint here and there, on hard stone-like foundations. Others were of hard oblong stones. Not natural, she felt sure. Made by someone. These had fared better.

Peering in, she saw few other remains—scraps of metal in odd shapes, much of it weathered and rusted. What these things had once been, she could not say.

Moving on down what had been a path—a hard path, she realized, because the ground was covered with something—she came to a building unlike the others. It was one small room, not many as the others were, and part of a roof remained, a clay-like substance, yet different from the oblong house-blocks. In front were some bent and rusted metal objects—large. Inside a scattering of metal objects, mostly small, made the place messy, but not impossible. If she could find something to sweep with. . . . She stepped to the door and then went around and looked behind. A small stream ran about fifty steps away, and some plants grew there—quite large. A few branches might act as a broom. More important, she realized, was the fact that she had been right: the land could be farmed. There was a place for her here, her own place.

She broke off some branches, swept the floor of the small house clean, and settled in. Only as she sat down to eat a bit of the food she carried did she realize how hard the floor was, however. Like the path, it was covered with something to make it flat and very solid.

Well, tomorrow she would work something out for sleeping inside on this hardness. For one more night she could sleep in the open. But this would be her house. She surveyed it with pride in the dwindling light. It was better than any house she had ever seen.

Full of hope and joy, she moved to a pleasant place near the stream, sheltered by a bit of the new growth. She drank her fill, ate some of the boy's vegetables raw, and fell asleep happy. Tomorrow a new life would begin.

She struggled awake soon after dawn, trying to remember where she was. It was morning. She had slept the whole night through. And where was she? She struggled to recollect. Then a glance showed her, and her delight returned. She was in a ruined city. In a place that was to be her very own. She sighed with pleasure, sure now that everything would be all right. If there were more problems, she could cope. The nagging thought that there might not be enough food for winter she poked inside. She would find a way. She would live. She had come this far, and she would survive.

Through the haze of her thoughts, she heard a noise. Was that what had awakened her? She listened carefully. There was something! A call! But there was no one here. She was sure there was no one here. She couldn't be disappointed, driven away again. And the ground was becoming fertile. Many could live here now. Maybe it wouldn't matter if there were others.

Slowly, cautiously, she lifted herself, seeking in every direction with her eyes.

The call came again. From far away. She lifted her

eyes to the hill she had run down. Was the caller over that way?

Yes, yes, on top. The boy. It had to be the boy. He had left his precious valley, his house, his farm. He had come seeking her. There was no one else he could be calling.

Her first instinct was to call back, to tell him she was here. Then she remembered: the fine house, the promise of food here. And it would be hers.

She fought within herself. Which was it to be? If she didn't call, the boy would never know she was here—would never come. She could make something that was hers alone.

Alone, that was it too. She would be as alone as the boy she had pitied, had scolded. Was it right to be so alone? Sometimes yes. But all the time? Never to see anyone, to speak to anyone, to hear a voice?

Looking up again, she saw him still standing, alone and dejected. She understood him. It was hard to make a decision thrust on you by someone else. She knew what he had been told, that no one must ever be allowed to stay. To cast aside a lifetime of teaching in one day was not easy. Perhaps, she thought again, no one had ever told him that girls sometimes came and sometimes were allowed to stay.

With a sudden inner joy, she called, "Boy, boy, here I am."

She saw his body turn, his feet spring down the hill as hers had last sunset. And she too, ran, ran to the foot of the hill. She'd show him the place she'd found, the house, and the good new growth. He'd know then that she came not out of mere hunger, not out of need for shelter, but out of wanting. He'd know she came as an equal. As one who wanted not simply a place, but a person. A sharing.

She smiled as he came up to her, threw his arms around her, startling her with the strength of his wanting. She knew then that he too, had suddenly seen the future alone and had rejected it.

She led him toward the house and the bush where her things were. Everything had worked out fine.

ENOGH

The following is a transcript of a broadcast made by Velta Akhbar on her eighty-fifth birthday. It was part of the Central Communications series for young people, "Ideas into Action."

First, I want to tell you that when they asked me to do this broadcast, I laughed. Me, Velta Akhbar, to talk about my life and about that old hack slogan, "Put Ideas to Work"? Absurd! They used that slogan when I was a child. And they didn't really believe it then. I can't imagine that they believe it now. It stirs up too much trouble.

When I said this, the Central Com people looked at me as if my mind were gone. And that made me laugh too. They were so earnest, those people from Central Com. Deliver me from the earnest! They never see beyond their noses. "Any child I've ever known who put ideas to work had trouble," I said. "It's time you stopped telling children things you don't mean. But if you want me to tell them the truth, then I'll do your broadcast." So here I am. And as you can see, I've at least started with the truth.

When I was a child, I was always putting ideas to

work. It was a mistake every time. Everybody hated it. Most of my ideas were for new ways of doing things. And even when they worked, they got me in trouble. Once, on the same day, I got an idea for a way to fold a leaf so it would sail through the air, using the breeze to bolster it up, and carry some small items on top. I folded and folded until I got it just right, then launched it, right into the path of old Mrs. Wokker, who was so frightened by this thing that sailed past, she nearly had a fit. She did fall and skin her knee. To get away from her, and my mother, I went off to finish an idea I had had for a new kind of pulley. The only decent place to try it was from the schoolhouse roof. It was nearly dark by the time I was ready, and no one could see me, so I climbed up, fastened the pulley, and started to pull my pet rabbit to the roof in a sling I had rigged up. Halfway up, the rabbit got scared and jumped through a window into the schoolhouse, where the town council was having a meeting. It didn't interrupt the meeting for long, but you would have thought I had caused an earthquake, the way everyone carried on. There was no encouragement there to "put ideas to work." And that was the way my life went as a child.

Was I never given any encouragement, people always ask when I tell them about my childhood? If not, how did you ever come to do so much? Well, I did get encouragement, in a negative sort of way. The more people encouraged me not to put ideas to work, the more I did it. I was just perverse, I guess. Or maybe I really liked the image I had created for myself. I was the town bad girl. And goodness knows what might have happened to me. My future was fairly uncertain at the time I came to school-leaving age.

That was just at the time the first sequesterings were being held. The Pre-Clordian Sweep Scientific Recovery Group had decided it needed young recruits. Our schoolmaster, along with four or five others, had been asked to bring one or two of his best—or most apt—students to a sort of camp where it could be seen if any of them showed the proper potential. This was done in several places where there were enough villages near a suitable location to make it practical. In those days people had to walk to any place they couldn't reach by boat.

The choice for the camp from our village was obvious—a young dolt named Dolbin. He was everybody's favorite. He always did the right thing. I hated him. And I wanted to go. This seemed my one chance to get help on some of my bigger projects, the ones I hadn't been able to carry out on my own. There was no one in the village who could, or would, help me. My small projects made trouble enough. But I was sure the Sweep people would be different.

I was persistent in those days, and I was determined. I had also discovered how the Central Com worked. Each village then had only one outlet. Generally some one person listened all day and spread the news to the rest of the village, though everyone came to listen to special programs. If there was a message to send from the village to some other place, the person in charge knew how to do that too. I had watched at the window of the house where all this was lodged in my village, until I knew not only what the operator did, but also something of how messages came in.

So at one point when the Central Com people were quiet, I was able to put my own message through to the machine. It said, "Velta Akhbar is to go to the Recovery Group sequestering next week." The operator, in fact the whole town, was so stunned by my message that no one stopped to ask how anyone outside the village had ever heard of me. I was notorious, they thought, known Earthwide.

As a result, it was just assumed that I was going. I think everyone was a little relieved. It meant a week without me. The only one really upset was Dolbin. He had been strutting around, airing his self-importance, because he had been chosen. Now I, who was always in trouble, was going too. It was a fine joke on him. Not the least of my triumph.

We set out on a fine morning, the three of us—the schoolmaster, Dolbin, and I—for a broad open meadow that lay almost a day's walk away in the middle of the Northeast Woods.

"I hope this trip will give you enough, Velta," my mother said as we left. "Enough what?" I asked. "Just enough," she said. And I was left to wonder what she meant. It irritated me that she had said something like that just as I was leaving. It was something I had to puzzle over, instead of using all my time on the way to think about the questions I wanted to ask and the projects on which I wanted help. For I was sure the people from the Recovery Group could do anything I wanted. After all, they had made the Central Com. I had confidence in them.

We walked through the woods, I saying nothing, dividing my thoughts between my projects and my mother's comment. The others kept to themselves too.

Maybe they were thinking of projects. Or maybe they were just content to walk and enjoy the day. That had never been my style.

When we arrived at the meadow, the two men from the Recovery Group who were to lead the camp were there, but none of the other schoolmasters or children had come yet. We were shown where to put our tents, and when they were up, were asked to help the men and the others, who had begun to arrive. I went to help the men. They were setting up a large tent, some cooking equipment, and some other gear they had pulled in on a cart, from a closer village than ours. A couple of times I saw easier ways to handle things and said so, but these men were no more eager to hear my ideas than anyone in the village. I couldn't believe it.

Enough! I said to myself. I've already had enough of this at home. I thought things would be different here.

But already I had discovered that these two men were not doers, not makers of things. They were local people whose job it was to take care of Recovery Group details in the area. And they did the best they could. I know that now. But that day I was mad clear through.

We had dinner finally. I met all the others. The sort of lot I should have expected. Mostly Dolbins, although a few seemed to have a spark of fun, at least. I did feel more at home in the group than I generally felt in my village. Most of these people at least understood what I was talking about when I asked some questions about the Central Com. Some of them had obviously studied it too. But I didn't think any of them had ever used it. Certainly none of them were at the camp under false pretenses because they had.

After dinner we had the first session. It was a time of quiet. Quiet, it seemed, was to be an important part of what we did at that camp, or sequestering, as they preferred to call it. We were supposed to think about what we wanted to get out of the experience. To plan for what we would bring home with us. To decide what things interested us most, what we wanted to do with our lives. I had answered some of those questions long before. My problem was that no one had ever agreed with me. No one really wanted me to put new ideas to work. Instead, they simply wanted me to work at ideas that had already been overworked, as far as I could see.

I went to bed disappointed. I think even I hadn't realized how much I had wanted this week to do for me. I couldn't sleep at first. I was desperate. *Enough,* my mother had said, and I wasn't going to get even a little. Yet, as I thought it over, I decided I could make something happen. I had done that before. And I'd do it again.

The next morning we had breakfast, and then the program began in earnest. First we had an introductory talk by one of the men, named Gwester. He explained the work of the Recovery Group, and I found myself interested. He said that, as we all knew, people had once lived on Earth who knew far more than we. They had developed all sorts of machines, most of which would be of little use to us. But some of their ideas and some of their inventions could be very helpful. The Recovery Group tried to find places where the records of these old people had been preserved.

From some of these records the idea for the Central Com had come. Now people were working on other ideas they had found, even some medical ones. We were, it seemed, not quite like those people. This fact fascinated me, and I would have begun to think about it if Gwester had not gone on to say that the one thing we really needed most was some kind of practical, reliable transportation on land. The Old Ones had had more kinds than they needed. But we had none, not even large animals, which had once served them well. Not enough had been discovered yet about how the Old Ones' mechanical transportation had worked to enable us to make something of our own.

"But why don't we just work something out for ourselves?" I asked. "Why wait to see what the Old Ones did?"

Gwester frowned at me. "Because we don't know enough theory. And we don't have enough people and resources to spend a lot of time learning," he said. That made sense. I decided Gwester was smarter than I had thought.

"But the Old Ones didn't have just exactly what we need," I went on. "And some things they had, we don't want. Don't we have to be ourselves?"

That was too much for Gwester. He would have none of that. All the answers lay with the Old Ones, he was sure. And I knew I couldn't disagree entirely. It did seem silly to try to invent something that had already been invented. Yet, if you couldn't find what you needed. . . .

I forgot what was going on around me, then. A transportation system! That was really a big idea. Could one really be developed? The idea was staggering. Not to have to walk everywhere over land. Not to have to carry on your back what you needed, or push or pull it in a wheeled cart. The Central Com had put us in touch with many places in the world. What if we could not only hear about all those far places, but see them as well? My mind reeled, and then went to work. They had to shout at me to tell me we were each supposed to find a quiet place and think about ourselves and what we wanted to do.

I was glad to have a little quiet. I had already begun to think. I drifted to the edge of the great clearing and sat down under a tree. Transportation. What was the answer? In those days I was convinced I could do anything. But the transportation problem was too big even for one morning, so gradually my mind drifted onto other things. I cursed the fact that I had been cheated again, and wondered how I could make the best of the week. Not by following the camp program, that was clear. At the same time, I didn't want to be sent home. If there was to be a lot of quiet, I could at least think in peace. Maybe I could get enough of that, though not enough of what I really wanted.

I looked around at the place where we were, then, more carefully than I had before. It was an odd place, a huge rectangle of grass—an open meadow, in the midst of a dense forest. An ideal place for a quiet retreat. It was as if someone had planned it, had cut away the trees in that vast shape. Yet I know no one had. Why would this happen?

Once again I was seeking an answer I couldn't quite grasp. What kept the trees from moving into the meadow? The ground was good. Would the dense

grass keep the seeds of the trees from rooting? Some
of them maybe, but not all. Surely a tree or two would
make its way in. Yet not one had. A few low bushes.
And yes, there was one lone tree. But it was small,
scrawny, pale. It looked as if it wasn't going to live
long. Was the soil below the grass roots, where the
tree roots would go, no good? Maybe. But why in so
regular a pattern?

When we were called for lunch, I asked Gwester if
he knew why this meadow was here, what made it so
regular in shape. Of course, he didn't. He hadn't even
thought about it. I should have expected that. But I
was disgusted just the same.

In the afternoon we were to wander around, get acquainted with the area, find plants and things that interested us, and ask questions about them. Gwester
and the other Recovery man, Syntron, would be waiting to explain what we had found. I laughed to
myself, wondering what kinds of questions they could
answer. Not mine, surely. Yet it was a fine day, a good
place. And with a little effort on my part, I would
have a maximum of freedom for a week. It had been
worth the effort of coming.

I spent the afternoon walking the edge of the forest.
There wasn't a break in the even pattern, except in
one place. There, the clearing moved a few paces into
the forest. That had to have some meaning. I mea-
sured that small space. Twenty steps up and down.
Six long steps across. All grassy, except for a few
bushes and an odd stone with plants on top. This was
the only place in the rim of the meadow where the
long straight sides were broken.

I brought no plants back to Gwester and Syntron.

And I didn't even mention the questions I had. Instead, I had decided to look for some answers myself. What would happen if I dug down below the sod? Would I find out what made the place so peculiar? It was an idea. And to put it to work, I told about the stone I had seen, the one with plants almost covering it; I proposed to dig out that stone and bring it in. And I did intend to do that; I just didn't say I also planned to dig a little deeper and see what lay below. Could I have a spade to use for my project? I asked.

The schoolmaster looked a little askance at my request. He knew me well enough to know that things were not always as they seemed with me. Yet, there wasn't much I could do with a spade. So he let it pass. And the next morning, I set off for my stone with the one spade available.

Most people had gone in another direction that day, looking for small stones to bring in. Each one was to go alone. By being alone, we were to face ourselves. We were all being taught to think for ourselves, choose for ourselves. My project fit in perfectly. What could be better than a stone with plants on top?

I began to dig around the stone to free it, and soon discovered it was bigger than it had seemed. It had been too well covered with growth for me to see it clearly. I dug deeper and deeper, and it soon became apparent that I might not be able to deliver it. I couldn't find the bottom of the stone, nor the edges. Below the soil it moved out in all directions.

At noon I went back and described my problem; but no one offered to help, and no one came to see. The others had become interested in their own projects. Some had begun plant collections to take home.

Others were trying to see how many small stones they could find on the forest floor. Still others were examining the trees to see how many varieties there were. No one else seemed concerned by the overall strangeness of the place, the uniqueness of where we were.

I went back alone, resolved to dig as deep as I needed to, to find the bottom of that stone. Something about it excited me. I felt that it had something to offer, even though I knew I could never carry it to the camp, to say nothing of home. Maybe I alone would have no memento of my week.

I dug until I thought I could dig no more. And then I did dig some more. Finally, I was in the hole, throwing the dirt out. By that time, I knew the stone was not a stone. It was some of the stone-like material the Old Ones had used. I had read about it. They made buildings, roads, everything with it. It was hard as stone, whatever they made it of. This was the first time I had seen it.

By dinnertime, I had discovered that my stone was connected to more of the stone-like material at a distance of almost my height below the soil. That had to be the reason no trees grew in all that huge rectangle. There was hard stone beneath it all. I was sure of it. But was there just a flat expanse of it—a playing field of some sort? Had it been the bottom of something? Or, was it maybe the top? I don't know where the later idea came from, it wasn't an idea that would have seemed logical to anyone else. We did not build underground. But I was overcome with it. I began to visualize a huge underground retreat. It was the most romantic idea I had ever had. I was in love with it at once.

I should have known better, but I raced back to the camp full of my thoughts. I had not yet learned to stop and think before I exploded with an idea that excited me. I told everyone what I had found, and what I had decided. And then realized that once more I had done it. I had put the wrong ideas to work. Everyone laughed. No one had ever heard such a strange tale. Dolbin began telling some of the things I had done at home. He didn't have to do it. He did it for free. And I was not grateful. I stormed at him, at everyone, trying to make them see. Until no one would even look at me. The schoolmaster took me aside and said he would send me home if he could. No good would come of my being there. He had always known that. He had no way of knowing why I had been asked, but he was sure it was a mistake. He was right, of course. But I had no intention of telling him so.

Gwester and Syntron, to their credit, were not so scornful as the others. They didn't offer to help, but they questioned me. I think they were afraid of committing themselves to what might be a scatterbrained idea. Yet they knew enough of the ways of the Old Ones to know that what I had suggested was not impossible.

So the next day I was allowed to pursue my project. The others went on with their collections. Insects had been added now. And some of the children had begun to think deeply about their futures. This was supposed to be the climax of the week. Each one of us was to have discovered her or himself by the time we left. And, supposedly, some one or two would have discovered a future with the Recovery Group. I was more interested in discovering the Old Ones. I still think it strange no one was even curious about what I had found. Yet maybe Dolbin's stories turned away those who might have come to look. I never knew.

I had decided how I would proceed. I would dig all around the stone that had started my work. I would discern its dimensions. If anything held the key to what lay below, I thought, that did.

First I cleared the top of the outcropping, my stone. When I looked at its hugeness I wondered what had ever made me think that I could carry it to camp. However, only a tiny bit of it, higher than the rest, had shown in the beginning.

Next, I worked my way down the sides, clearing evenly as I went, until on one side I saw a piece of metal, fastened to the stone. It had been put there at some time by some person. I was sure of it. My excitement was almost more than I could bear. There were words on the metal, words I did not understand, and an arrow. Below, as I hastily uncovered more, I found a big piece of metal, a kind of door.

Was that what it was? And if so, how did it open? More arrows—these painted in colors on the rock—so faint they were hardly visible any longer, pointed to a small additional piece of metal set in the stone. It was just a round place, with no writing. I touched it, to see what it felt like, and suddenly there was a noise. I jumped back.

A rattle, then some sounds as if a great monster was awakening inside. And slowly, almost as if it wasn't going to happen, the little door slid open. Would it stay open? I put my head through. Steps lay ahead, down into the dark. Again there was a button and arrows, these far more visible, as if they had been waiting for me to see them. I pushed the button, and the stairs below were lighted.

Did I dare go down? What would happen to me if the door closed, or the light went off when I could no longer see the door, even if it stayed open? Yet how could I not take a chance? I stepped in, then gingerly crept down the stairs. It was foolish of me. I can say that now. I think I knew it even then. But I had never been a careful child.

At the foot of the stairs a long corridor opened. Many doors lay along that corridor. I opened the first I came to and saw a bed, a chair, a comfortable room. Yet everything was old. If I touched something, it would surely fall apart, I thought. Yet when I did touch something, it felt firm. Being shut up in a dry place had preserved everything, but I didn't know that then. I crept to the next door and found the same. People had lived here!

I grew bolder. Stole on until I came to a door that opened into a very large room. I had never seen an inside place so enormous. Our whole village could have fit in just that one vast hall! And it was all lighted somehow. With what I did not know. I stood on a high balcony, and below me were machines. Some like birds. Others tall—rockets, I can say now. The sight frightened me, awed me, fascinated me. I could have stood and looked all day. It was long past lunchtime, but I gave that no thought. I moved on. Beyond the huge room—far, far down the corridor— was a room lined with books. This is where it is, I thought. This is where I can find out. And for once I agreed with someone else. Why work something out for myself, if someone had already done it for me? Could I learn to read those books, learn those languages? Oh, yes, if someone would only let me, I could. I knew I could. To do that would be enough.

I spent the whole afternoon with those books. I couldn't read what they said, but I could look at the pictures and marvel. Suddenly, I realized how late it must be, and I hurried back down the corridor, past the big room, past the sleeping rooms, and up the stairs. At the top of the stairs, I pushed the button and the lights went out. Outside I saw that it was indeed late in the day. On the chance that if I pushed the outside button again it would close the door, I touched it, and the door slid down, with the same heavy rumble.

Now I had a new problem. Should I tell what I had found? It was so big a question that for once I took some time to plot a sensible answer. I had found myself in those hours underground. I had found my life, if anyone would let me have it. And I didn't want to spoil my chances. What was I to do?

I couldn't tell everyone. They had had their chance and missed it. But I must tell someone. I couldn't not. This was too important. It wasn't just for me. The knowledge a lot of people might need could be in those books. So after dinner I told Gwester. He was the one who had talked about the knowledge of the Old Ones. He was the one who might understand, I thought.

At first he didn't believe me. We sat apart from the others, where he had reluctantly come at my insistence. But as I went on, I think he couldn't believe that anyone could make up such a story. He agreed to come with me the next morning. He said nothing to anyone else, nor did I.

In the morning he casually set out with me, saying he wanted to see where I had been digging. We entered the underground chambers in the same way I had entered the day before. And all was as I had said. I told him then how I felt. What I longed to do. And once more he listened. He even said he thought something could be done for me.

We spent the day in that underground place, exploring. The light was electric, he said. But he didn't know how it could possibly still work, after so many years with no one there. It was something to find out, I decided.

Some of the machines were transportation. They were meant to fly in the air, we decided. People on Earth now would never agree to that. Even to me it seems a bit obscene. But those machines started me thinking. If I could find out what made them go. . . .

It was many years before I finally invented what did become the Mechanized Transport. But my ideas for it began that day. I have put ideas to work. I have done it all my life. But as you can see, it wasn't popular when I was young. And I suspect it's still not popular for some of you.

We told no one at the camp of the discovery. It seemed better that no one know until the area could be protected in some way. A few days later we were all back in our villages, and Gwester and Syntron were in a place where they could send a message to the Recovery Group headquarters. Eventually those who really knew about the Old Ones came to explore, and they came to me too. My sequestering was supposed to have been a failure. I had brought nothing back as Dolbin had. A waste, people had said. But when my mother asked if it had been enough, I had said, "Yes, enough. At least I hope it will be."

And when the new people came from the Recovery Group and took me back to the meadow, back to that library, and taught me to discover what was in those books, she understood, I knew.

It was enough. And yet, never enough. For there is always something ahead. I don't want to make things anymore, not as I did when I was young. Things are not so important to me now. Not even the Mechanized Transport. Now I feel that ideas, themselves, are more important than the work they lead to or the things they create. Things put to work are important only when they free us for ideas. It may be that all those others there during that sequestering week knew this, knew then what I have come to know only in these last years. Yet I do not regret my life.

Put ideas to work. That phrase still makes me laugh. Yet it has been my life. And I have loved it. It's enough for me, whether others like it or not.

ACCORD

Casselia Sorchum had never wanted to travel. At least not to another planet. No one on Earth had ever wanted to travel that far. She kicked at the plastic floor of the terrace and a little dust blew into her face, from her motion and from the wind that was always on the move on Clord. The few specks of dust were very like the dust of home. They reminded her of how absurd it was to be in a place where the only thing that seemed like home was dust. Yet Earth was more light-years away than she cared to think. And she had no idea of when she might return. She kicked at the plastic again. This time there was no dust.

Clordians were like the wind that blew around their planet, she thought. Always on the move. Busy. And yet she couldn't see that it got them anywhere. To places, yes. But they never got down into things. They were always racing off without having really seen the place they had been. And with all that racing around, their children never went on a sequestering. At least she didn't think they did. She'd never actually had a chance to talk to any of them. If they didn't go sequestering, it was no wonder they were so restless; they had never had to face themselves, these people, never had to find out what they were. Never learned to focus. That had to be what made all the Clordians she knew so thrusting and jumpy. She didn't like them.

"Casselia!"

Casselia sighed. It was her mother, with more instructions, she was sure, for the stupid banquet they were going to tonight. Another one! The third in a week. It used to be that she hadn't had to go. Which was much better. She hated banquets. Staying at home in this too-confined apartment might be lonely, but at least she didn't have to flutter and smile at all those Clordians. She had never had to say much to them; her parents had always said she should be as quiet as possible. But just being with them was unpleasant. They seemed to shove at you so.

"Remember, Casselia, we are envoys. We represent our entire planet here on Clord. We must not take our responsibility lightly." She had heard that too often. And she had seen too often what it meant. A strange, quiet retreat. Her parents behaved differently, were not themselves, when they were with the Clordians. She hated to watch them. It didn't seem necessary. They weren't owned by Clord, not yet, anyway.

Casselia made a face to herself as she walked from the terrace into the impossibly rigid and ridiculously orderly apartment she and her mother and father had been given for their "brief visit." Apartment! It was just a fancy name for a prison. The three of them were always being watched. She was glad her parents didn't even try to pretend that the Clordians weren't most interested in knowing if Earth was safe, or if the people of Earth were likely to make new problems for

Clord. Everyone on Earth had known the Clordians would want to investigate thoroughly after a spaceship from Clord had gotten in trouble and landed on Earth.

The only question Earth people had had was what the Clordians would do. A Clordian research team—ambassadors of friendship—had arrived soon after, which was expected. But they had stayed only a few days, which was unexpected. There had been no attempt at a takeover, though surely they had seen that the people of Earth had no weapons. The Clordians had simply come, asked for an ambassador to accompany them home, and then gone. It was they, the Sorchums, who had been chosen to go. So here they were, ambassadors. And Casselia hated it. Had hated every day of the four absurd fifty-day Clordian months they had been there.

"Casselia! Hurry!"

"I'm here," she answered, strolling through the door to the gathering room, where her mother was standing. "Why do I have to go? You never let me say anything. I just smile. And all those heavy-handed clods pat me on the head. I never see anyone my own age. And nobody ever pays any attention to me."

The atmosphere as she made her usual complaint was not the usual patient-but-tense "do as we say." As she walked up to her mother, there was more of a smile in the air, not the half-formed sense of dread she so often caught from her parents. Her mother was thumbing absently through the clothes in a huge wall wardrobe—some Clordian-style clothes, some Earth clothes.

"Sit down," she said.

Casselia slid into one of the slippery Clordian chairs and waited, perplexed. Something had changed. There was a sureness in her mother. It hung all over the glossy surface of the room like an alien skin. Not that the three of them had ever been really unsure of themselves inside. They were what they were, most of the time; yet there was something new today.

"I think you should wear this dress of mine, this Earth dress, to the dinner with the Commander of All the Clords tonight."

"Oh, Mother, not him," Casselia began, before she took in all her mother had said. A grown-up dress! And an Earth dress! She hated the Clordian clothes she usually wore to dinners. Clordians were built differently, and no matter how their clothing styles were altered, their clothes simply didn't fit Earth people. The dress her mother held out was the one thing in her mother's wardrobe she had always wanted to try on.

"You're about my size now, you know," her mother went on, as if she hadn't seen Casselia's surprise. "You've grown a lot in the year and a half since we left Earth."

She's giving me a chance to recover, Casselia thought. There was something going on.

"Let's try it," her mother said. "Of course, if you'd rather wear one of your own dresses, you can." The look on her face said she knew better.

The dress fit just as Casselia had known it would. She'd often wondered why her mother had brought it. It wasn't like the things she usually wore. In fact she'd never had it on. Never had it on! Had it been brought for her?

"It was for me. You brought this for me!" She turned to her mother almost accusingly. "Did you bring it for tonight? How could you know?"

"I brought it for you to wear when the right time came," her mother said. "And that time has come, I think." The sureness Casselia had sensed before still filled her mother's voice.

"Does this mean I don't have to be a child anymore? That I can talk?" she asked hopefully. She had, after all, had her sequestering before she left Earth. And she could focus better than anyone she knew. She was not a child, although they had persisted in treating her like one on this trip. She wasn't full grown, of course, but she had a right to more consideration than she had had.

She sighed, thinking as she often had before that she'd had more sequestering than most, but had never had a chance to try out its benefits. Even her curiosity was hedged about by rules. On the long trip here, they'd made her stay in her small room, except for exercise and times with her parents. Her mother had taught her the same things she would have learned at school. But she'd been alone so much. No friends, no one her own age to talk to. No one to explore with. She'd actually looked forward to arriving in Clord, in the hope that she might see more people. She'd even had the notion that she might go to a school here. But life on Clord had been much like life on the spaceship. There'd been lots of time to think, lots of time to become herself. Lots of time to develop her inner unity. Too much time. You needed people too, in the end, to find out what you were and to learn what was really true.

"Can I talk tonight?" she asked. "Really talk? I can speak Clordian. I won't make any stupid mistakes."

Her mother nodded. "Say what you will, when you will. But," she added softly, "remember why we are here. The Earth depends on us. And yet not on us so much, I think, as on the slender thread of what we all are as individuals and as a people. And you, Casselia, are Earth, the Earth the Clordians want to know, as much as any. More than many, perhaps, for away from Earth we see its delights, its wonders most clearly, enjoy them most thoroughly. Be what you are, and let the winds of Earth run through you."

"Earth is fifty light-years away," Casselia murmured. "Ten months of travel."

"But not far in your thoughts."

"No, always there."

"Then be of Earth, and be it fully. You are not yet a woman, Casselia, not yet fully grown; but tonight you must be the best of us. That's all I can tell you, and by the Guardians, I hope it's enough." A flit of worry crossed her face. Then she smiled again, and turned to select a dress for herself.

The best of us. The thought was frightening. Why her? And so all-at-once when she had hardly opened her mouth before. She had been the unheard child forever, there on demand but quiet. Now all of a sudden she was to be the "best of us." And with the worst of them, as far as she was concerned. Well, maybe not the very worst. The Clordians were all so heavy. That was the only word—*heavy*. They didn't seem to have any sense of discovery. When they came into a room, they just came. They blunted in. And they said things without knowing what they said. She had envied them once. It had seemed so easy. She had thought they didn't care. But now she knew they did; they just didn't see what lay below the surface of things. And it made her feel sorry. They did awful things to each other.

"They're so heavy to handle," she said, voicing a part of her thoughts to her mother.

Her mother smiled, in the same warm carefree way she had shown earlier.

"Just be yourself," she said again. "But be all you are. Remember all you know. That will be enough, I think."

It was so confusing. Casselia pushed her thoughts aside and looked at the dress again. Why couldn't her mother be more specific? Be all she was . . . what, by the Guardians, did that mean?

When the time came to go, she was nervous. It was strange to feel that way. She never had. Her parents smiled and talked in the air car, and she felt better after a bit. Her father was as light and confident as her mother, and that gave her further support. It was almost as if they were at home on Earth. The guardedness she had seen in them here was gone. Her father hadn't joked like this since they'd climbed on the spaceship. She tried to share their mood, but didn't quite make it; she couldn't look forward to the evening as they seemed to be doing. Dinner parties on Clord were so somber, so stiff and proper. What she really wanted was fun. And she didn't think this was going to be.

As usual, the dinner was to be out-of-doors. Even though the air held no sparkle, the ground was fake, and most plants everywhere had been trimmed into shapes beyond all recognition as living things, the Clordians seemed to like getting out of their all-the same rooms into their almost all-the-same gardens. The garden at the palace of the Commander of All the Clords, she saw to her surprise, had some real ground, well plasticized to prevent dust, but real ground nevertheless. The trees had been trimmed into the shapes of long extinct Clordian animals. The bushes too. All carefully placed in very geometric patterns. The last garden she had been in had had only bushes—cut and trimmed into little buildings. This was a bit better. The tables were set down one long aisle between huge lizard-like creatures of trees, and small rodent-like bushes, alternating on either side. Stiff, stiff!

Casselia looked at the sky and wished it would rain. That would be really different. It never rained on Clord. She wasn't sure, but she thought it had never happened there. The water was all under the ground. Or maybe she'd heard that some clouds sometimes did hold water, but they were drained and the water stored. Certainly nothing was ever left to chance on Clord. It was a pity. Casselia sighed. A little rain would do a lot for one of these state occasions.

There were evidently not to be as many guests tonight as usual. Only a dozen tables for ten, instead of the customary thirty or forty tables. There were always representatives from conquered and dependent planets who had to be included. Whether the smaller size boded good or ill, she decided, might depend on who was invited to a smaller dinner. Were all Clordians old? Surely not. Then why did she have to come if no young Clordians ever did?

Walking between her mother and father, she was conscious of many eyes upon her, a staring look even from those who had seen her many times before. What was happening? She looked down at her dress, not really sure now that she was ready to be grown-up. At home it would be fine. But here? What did it mean? Her mother had never been so secretive before. And telling her only to be herself, instead of going into one of those long lectures she always gave before a dinner. When was she to be herself? And how could she really be herself here? Suddenly she felt nervous again. Something was obviously expected of her tonight, and she didn't know what. She felt very much alone.

Her mother smiled at her, as if she knew, and the fear and the aloneness retreated a little. But not the question. What was she expected to do?

The Commander of All the Clords was coming. A dreary bore. Almost the worst of the Clordians, she thought again. Yet in many ways she felt sorry for him too. He tried so hard to be nice—to express what seemed to be real regret about what had happened so long ago. He seemed to be obsessed with the past. Too much so, she thought. No matter what he said, he would do the same thing again if it seemed necessary to him. He was afraid of Earth. Odd, wasn't it? The Clordians had so much power—and yet so little knowledge. They couldn't see beyond themselves and their own ways; couldn't really cope with the unexpected. People on Earth had been almost too much of a shock.

"Ah, my great good friends, the honorable envoys, Sorchum. And you, my dear—Casselia, is it not? How elegant you are tonight. You are becoming a fine young woman among us. We are honored."

The Commander held up his hands to touch those of her parents, and then turned to her. She moved her hands up slowly and with reluctance. She had never had to do this before. No one had really noticed her, except to pat her on the head. The big hands came forward toward hers and stopped. Realizing she would have to observe the silly custom, she poked her hands on and touched his.

Looking at his face for a moment, she caught an expression of surprise, instead of the customary stony smile. What had surprised him? Maybe something behind her that she couldn't see. But what could possibly surprise the Commander of All the Clords at one of these machine-made dinners? She turned to look, and to her amazement a young man was coming down the avenue—a boy, really, not much older than she, by Clordian standards. Glancing back, she saw that the Commander was smiling again. It must be all right then. And what a relief to know that Clordians were sometimes young.

"You see him," said the Commander of All the Clords, smiling as real a smile as she had ever seen him give. "Then come meet him. It is time you knew our Vester."

Casselia looked up at her parents, who nodded, pleased, and let her follow the Commander alone. She was to meet a young Clordian at last. She regretted that he was in uniform. It seemed to limit his possibilities. But never mind. He was young. And that was enough for now.

"Casselia Sorchum, Vester Wrang. Vester is the son of my son, one you may have heard of." His face held a proud look. "The one who alone convinced the

Southeast Quadrant that it should be a part of us, accept our protection."

Casselia shuddered. She'd heard. The Southeast Quadrant was a new territory for Clord. They were about to give it the "advantages" of Clordian ownership and protection. She barely managed to smile at Vester. The thought struck her that he might be worse than nothing. How could she be herself with the son of the conqueror of the Southeast Quadrant? Yet he was young. And something new had to happen to her or she'd explode.

"Why don't you two young people find a place to get acquainted?" A smile covered the Commander's face, but his words were really a command. The smile on Vester's face was too wide.

"Be yourself," her mother had said. And suddenly, unaccountably, the lightness that had held her parents seized her. She was tired of the whole dreary business, but she'd show them that she could be all she knew. She focused her thoughts on Vester and grinned, which gave her the satisfaction of seeing both the Commander and his grandson look startled.

"Marvelous," she said. "I'm delighted to meet you, Vester. What about that bench over there?"

He looked a bit dazed as she moved confidently to the bench. But he came. His face, however, seemed a bit blue.

"Have you ever been to Earth?" she asked sweetly, knowing he hadn't. There had been only two ships of Clordians on Earth, as far as she knew, and only one of any consequence. Sequestered as she had been on the return journey of that second ship, she had still seen everyone aboard and knew that Vester had not been among them. None of them had been young.

Numbly he shook his head. He seemed to be a little dizzy. Maybe he hadn't been prepared for this meeting either. Did young Clordians not go to fancy dinners at all? If they didn't, he might be even more dazed than she, though she had never noticed any Clordians before who seemed weak and ineffectual in any situation. Blunt, yes. And driving. But never weak. Or were young Clordians different? Were they kept apart from others—at least from adults—until they had that hard outside? Of course, she had never really spoken to adult Clordians either, just observed them. Yet it was strange that he didn't say anything. The only thing to do seemed to be to go on.

"I'm very fond of Earth, though Clord is nice too," she added quickly. She concentrated on him, trying to bring him out of his quiet, to make him a part of the place and the event, as she'd been taught to do. "We're comfortable here. Your people have provided well for us," she added hastily at his look of lost amazement. "Though I sometimes miss our out-of-doors. I went on my sequestering almost two years ago now. That's when you go off alone to discover yourself. I spent three days in a canyon by a little stream. I found some old bottles that my mother said might have been made before the Clordian Sweep."

That was a mistake, especially when his grandfather felt so embarrassed about it. "We're not sure but what it didn't help us in the end, the Clordian Sweep," she said, trying to recoup her error. "We're different now, the scientists say. And maybe better." She stopped short as a pale green color swept over Vester's face.

What was wrong? Was it the Clordian Sweep still? That had been a mistake. Should she talk about something he knew more about?

"I wish I could see more of Clord. There hasn't been much chance for me to get out. And I haven't met anyone young before. You can't imagine how glad I am to get to know you. I haven't talked to anyone my own age in a whole Earth year and a half. And everyone needs someone to talk to, not just parents."

Vester remained silent. Would nothing bring him out? Could he talk at all? His color was now pale mauve. She wondered briefly if he had ever seen a rainbow. No, of course not, unless he had traveled away from Clord, and that didn't seem likely if he was as much of a lump as he seemed. Yet she was supposed to be the best of Earth for him! This must have been what her mother meant. This whole thing was so obviously planned. Did that mean she was supposed to get Vester to talk? Was it some kind of test? She felt a moment's panic, then decided to throw caution to the winds. Earth was what she really wanted to talk about, so that was what she would talk about.

"Do you go on sequestering? I think about mine all the time. It was really beautiful there. There was a gorgeous rainbow while I was in the canyon. You've never seen one, I guess. It's an arch in the sky, and it's all colors. From the rain and the sun. The sun, that's our star. I had never seen such a perfect rainbow. But it wasn't just that it was so perfect, it was that it happened while I was there."

She remembered it very clearly. It had been a sort of promise, of what she did not know. Lost in thought, she stopped talking a moment. The rainbow had been the answer then. She had been seeking deep inside, as she'd been taught, for a strong inner unity, for a sense of direction, and suddenly she'd known that for her it would always come from seeing and holding steady one thing outside herself. Her director had said later that that was a bit of oversimplification, but it would do until she moved on.

Thainking back still to that moment, she held Vester in her gaze and decided to put her discovery to work at last. She'd concentrate on Vester as if he were a double rainbow, even though he seemed to have no voice at all. How could the Clordians have done so much, when their young people couldn't even hold up one end of a conversation?

"What is your school like? Do you have to find a focus, a unity, as we do? Do you have to explore and discover? Or do you just learn facts and things, as we do sometimes? My mother's taught me a lot on the spaceship and here, but the exploring has been a bit limited. What I'd really like is to go to school with others again. It's more fun. Do you go to school?" She smiled the brightest smile she had and gave Vester the full force of it.

He fainted. At least he slumped over and fell to the ground.

Startled, she gave a short scream. What had she done? Surely her conversation wasn't so dull it put people into a dead faint. She'd never had that trouble at home. And if what she was saying was so bad, why hadn't he changed the subject? Why hadn't her parents warned her, told her what to talk about? She reached down to lift his head, but other hands reached him first, motioned to her to move, and stretched him out on the bench. There had been people closer than she had realized. The Commander and her parents and several others.

"I don't know what happened," Casselia said, puzzled more than ever. "He just fainted."

The Commander looked at her sternly, accusingly. But it didn't matter to her. She was too upset. The first young Clordian she'd seen, and it had gone so badly. Was she going to be alone forever?

"He never said anything," she murmured, trying to understand. "He turned all sorts of colors and then he fainted."

The Commander looked at her for a second, turned white, and took a step toward Vester, where he lay on the bench.

Casselia took a few quick steps toward her parents, needing them. It was a relief to find that they were not worried or even angry. The Clordians around them were so upset. The air was all stirred up. But her parents were an island of peace and, yes, gaiety—the same laughing gaiety she had sensed earlier, though on the outside both seemed concerned and sober. She had never seen them this way with Clordians before.

"This is most unusual. And most unexpected," said the Commander of All the Clords ominously. "You must understand, my dear Sorchums, that Vester is in perfect health. He has never had the least problem. We were all watching. We saw nothing. But he is my heir. You know, of course, that we must examine the girl."

Casselia looked at her parents. Were they going to let that happen? She'd only talked at the boy. Silly thing! What weaklings the Clordians were if they couldn't even take a little conversation.

"We understand," her father said, speaking directly at the Commander, in a way she had not seen her father speak on Clord before. The withdrawal, the hesitation were gone. It was, in fact, the Commander who was withdrawing. "It will be simply a superficial physical examination, I assume, to make sure she has no concealed weapon. And we will be allowed to be present."

The Commander of All the Clords rubbed his hand over his eyes. "Yes, of course," he said, almost softly.

What a strange turn of events. Walking slowly between her parents, who in turn walked between the precisely trimmed trees and bushes, she gave up for the third time that day. Once more she didn't know what was going on.

Before the curious stares of the other guests, a little parade wound its way toward the sheath building at the head of the garden. Vester and his bearers were first, then Casselia and her parents, then two guards, then the Commander of All the Clords, and then two more guards.

We need a little music, Casselia thought, and almost giggled. She glanced at her parents and somehow had the idea they were thinking the same. All three shared a smile. Good, then they weren't worried. But why? She didn't have a weapon, of course, and they knew it. But the Clordians could do anything in that building and no one would ever know, no one on Earth, at least. The building didn't even have any windows. She drew herself up very straight. She would not be afraid.

The march continued slowly, moving deliberately toward the door. Nearer, Casselia felt a sudden moment of panic, but her mother, probably feeling her tense up, squeezed her hand and said softly, "Remember the Earth. Focus on those who come to you here. Be concerned for them and not for yourself. Yet be yourself. Relax and be easy." Another smile. From her father too. She relaxed.

She could do that all right. Her focus was fine. And the Earth was always hard to forget. It was winter at home now; hard to imagine in the everlasting sameness of Clordian weather. The bite of cold came to mind and she held it there, willing away the present. Then she dropped the thought. It was the present that needed her concentration.

They were inside the door. Soft lights were everywhere and nowhere. The eternal hard chairs of Clord gave way here to a few with some upholstery, but only a few. It was nevertheless, she realized, a fine home. The home of the Commander of All the Clords. Of course, it would be fine. But why was she here, and in such a predicament?

A woman came in then, glanced at Casselia where she and her parents had stopped, and moved to Vester. She looked down at him, shook her head, and led the bearers down the hall beyond.

"You understand that further association may now be impossible—certainly it is unlikely that we can look for a marriage—but of course any action depends on what we find."

Casselia looked up, startled. She had not seen the Commander come over, busy watching Vester disappear.

"Marriage?" she murmured, almost without thinking.

"She doesn't know?" he asked quickly.

Her parents shook their heads.

"We had not agreed to it, nor, of course, had she. It was better to see how the meeting went. Such things cannot be forced, especially under such abnormal circumstances. Obviously it could never be a true marriage, only a marriage of state."

"Cannot be forced," the Commander puffed. "But such things, even under these circumstances, are expected. No force is needed. I myself have many wives from other planets."

"Which is just the point," murmured her mother. "On Earth, marriage when it occurs is never expected. It simply is. But once a true marriage comes about, both parties have a right to expect something of each other. Formal agreements are not enough for us. We cannot live in patterns."

The Commander did not reply.

Casselia looked at the floor, then up at her parents. Had they expected her to like him? To marry Vester? Had they wanted it? Would that protect Earth from Clord? Be yourself, they had said. And she had been. That Vester was a limp old toadstool! He'd never said a word. And then he'd fainted. How could she marry that? Besides, she was too young. And more than that, she wanted to go home. Vester would never fit in on Earth. They'd as much as said that a marriage between an Earth person and a Clord person wouldn't really work. So why did they want her to have that kind of marriage?

"If you want my thoughts, it was a silly plan," she

said, looking up at the Commander of All the Clords defiantly. "I never would have come tonight if I had known. I don't intend to marry for at least ten Earth years and maybe never. Nobody has to. And that Vester is a. . . ." She stopped. It might be best not to voice her opinion of him to his grandfather. She'd probably said enough already.

She looked up to see if she had offended him too much and discovered that his face was almost as colorful as Vester's had been. He seemed about to explode. What right had he to feel that way, no matter who he was?

Focusing on him, angry now beyond caring, she exploded first. "Who do you think you are, pushing people around? We all have a right to be just what we are, and you can't make us anything else."

The Commander was suddenly white.

"Casselia," her mother cautioned lightly, "better calm down. Save yourself for the two ladies here."

The Commander dropped to a padded chair as two women, large and burly, approached.

"Are you the girl to be searched?" one asked, not unkindly.

Casselia nodded. But as the woman put out a hand to take her, she felt a sudden return of her earlier fears and anger; she gazed at the woman stonily, wishing her away. The woman's hand did not touch her.

"Well, come on," said the other, shoving the first aside.

That woman's hand reached out, and as Casselia turned her attention there, it dropped also.

"Perhaps," said her father quietly, "if you'd lead us

to the room you wish, we could follow. That might be easier for you." He took Casselia's hand, and they both looked at the women.

"I'm not going to touch her," said the second woman, backing away. She turned and all but ran from the room, the first woman following.

"Perhaps you should get some other women," Casselia's father murmured to one of the guards who stood near the Commander. "Those seem to behave strangely."

The guard did not move.

"No one will come now," another guard said. "Something peculiar here. It's better not to find out. We know what we know. And that's good enough."

"Yes, it is good enough," Casselia's father said. "Clord is a great empire. It is the greatest we know. You have much to be proud of. And we are pleased to have been among you and to have had this chance to learn your ways. They are not our ways, but we all have a right to accept what we will and to let others enjoy what they will."

He meant it, Casselia saw. He was trying to smooth over a hard moment for the Clordians. And yet the meaning of it all still wasn't quite clear. What had she done? She was sorry she had shown fear and anger, and would apologize if the women came back. Yet why had they gone away? Surely in their job they had had people afraid before. She'd heard that fear was a defense. But you had to do something with it beside focus on the person, didn't you? Or didn't you? Something had happened to everyone she had focused on today. Was there something in her?

"I'm sorry," she said, looking at her father. "I didn't

mean to be afraid. I didn't mean to drive her away, if I did. Did my focusing do it?"

"Casselia, don't be sorry," said her mother. "You did only what any of us might have done in your place."

Her mother still wasn't angry and neither was her father. The light feeling remained. The joy and warmth of Earth.

The Commander of All the Clords lifted his head now, although it seemed an effort for him. "We have no records to indicate that any of the people of Earth were . . . well, were as this child seems to be."

"Your records are from a time long past," said Casselia's father. "And the child is not alone. We are all the same, it is just that we who know our strength have learned to mask it. It is an inheritance, perhaps, from your ancestors."

"You were changed—by what we did?" whispered the Commander.

"Perhaps. Or perhaps this power is something we always had and only developed after your coming," said Mr. Sorchum. "We have found old medical records, and there is much in them that does not agree with what we find in ourselves today. We are seldom ill, seldom even injured. We do not multiply rapidly. And we seem to have an affinity for and a power over the other living things on Earth. Yet we have small effect on each other, perhaps because we do not care to have, perhaps because we neutralize each other. We have done no research on the matter, because we know so little of it ourselves. We simply know we have a force, an energy, within ourselves that may have many uses. Only recently have some of us begun to learn its control. A few adults have been experimenting. But we all have the power and can use it in crude ways. And we are sure that what one can do alone, many can do together."

"How did we land?"

"We wanted you to land. We were as curious as you. Partly because we did not really know the extent of our strength. We were not sure until you came, until we could test ourselves quietly against you. Only a few of us knew enough of what we might possibly be able to do to be a part of the test. So you saw only those who could control their powers, test them in unfelt ways."

"But why should the girl damage the boy? What had he done?"

"She did not mean to do anything but speak. She didn't know what we know about the power of focusing. At home it is a polite thing to do. You focus on those to whom you speak. And because she sensed the importance of the meeting, she focused her full attention on him. He simply was unprepared for the energy that she was beaming toward him."

"Why did you let it happen if you knew?" the Commander barked, almost himself again.

"I didn't know what would happen myself. We none of us know just how we measure in this thing. Casselia has been kept apart because we did not dare expose her to others too soon. My wife and I needed to test you first. We had to have time before we revealed what we knew, time to find out the extent of our powers. We needed the chance to do this as much as you needed two or three envoys from Earth to study."

"What have you learned? How strong is it?" the Commander pressed on.

"We are not wholly sure yet. To know the whole of the matter, we would have to test openly, and that would be too dangerous, for you more than us, I suspect."

Casselia looked at her parents in amazement. Was all this really true? And why hadn't she known it? But was it true? No. Only some of it was. And some of it might be. They were bluffing. There was a power there. And they had known, had hoped, at least, that it would help. They had given her all the strength they could, and then hoped it would be enough. And it had been. Her mother gave a small smile that said she was right. She knew her mother well enough for that. What would happen next? It didn't matter, she guessed, as long as the Clordians knew for sure that some power existed. It was marvelous! She wanted to laugh.

"You should be wiped out," the Commander was saying.

"We cannot be wiped out. We three perhaps, but not, we are sure, a whole, focusing Earth. It is possible that no spaceship will ever land again, or even come close, without the consent of Earth. In our absence, no one will be allowed to land. No spaceship will touch Earth until we have returned.

"All Earth now knows something of what has been discovered. Every child on Earth has been taught to focus for years. It's been a way of learning things quickly and of complimenting your friends. Now it may be a defense as well."

The Commander dropped his hands to his side. "Will the boy recover?" he asked.

"I think he will," murmured Mrs. Sorchum. "I hope so."

"And what is to be done?" The Commander seemed confused.

"Nothing," said Casselia's father. "We exist, we of Earth, and we have a right to be. There are five hundred planets in all the Clords, and we want none of them. We have our own problems. And they are not problems of going beyond ourselves. Not yet, and probably not ever. We are no threat to you. Except that we exist apart from you. And you surely know that we are not alone in that."

"You know that too," the Commander whispered, as if a great secret had been spoken. This time Casselia felt he was truly afraid, more afraid than he had been of them. And she understood his fear. They, the people of Earth, were the first minded beings he had actually encountered who could not be talked or fought into becoming a part of Clord. One such planet might be tolerated. But if there were others, and he had to admit it, then Clord would never seem as powerful again.

"We have seen ships in the sky that were not Clordian," said her father. "None have landed. It may be that we have driven them away, unknowing. Or perhaps they have not needed to land to see what we are. Yet they have been there, and we have seen them."

"I knew . . . I felt sure . . . Reports have said . . . Soon it will all end for us, I know." The Commander was dejected beyond reason, Casselia thought. Who needed an empire? Earth didn't have one, and it was better by far than Clord.

"No, no," she said, focusing her thoughts on him, "don't feel that way. There's room for all of us. You can't just disappear. We might even come to like you." Surprised at herself, she drew back. She'd forgotten that you couldn't focus on a Clordian. But she had meant what she said.

"In my school they tell a joke," she said hestitantly, looking away. "They say, 'And who is Earth's greatest enemy?' 'Clord,' everyone says. And then they say, 'And who is Earth's greatest friend?' 'Clord,' everyone says. 'Why?' they ask. 'Because they're the only ones we have to talk to beside ourselves, and who on Earth can live without talking?' It's a kind of silly joke. Not all of us talk a lot." She ended rather lamely. On Clord it didn't make as much sense, somehow, as it did on Earth. Clordians didn't have the same feeling of all being one as people on Earth did.

The Commander, however, gave her a weak smile. "How hungry are you?" he asked unexpectedly.

Casselia gave a start. She hadn't thought of that. But now that the question had come up, she knew that she was starved.

"I could eat," she said truthfully.

"Then let's go to dinner, if you'll just concentrate on the food."

The Commander bowed, and she stepped beside him. Together they moved out the door and down the rows of trees and bushes to the tables. Her parents followed; and the other guests, who had been waiting outside the door, fell in. The dinner was somewhat overdone, but Casselia didn't care. She had the feeling that life on Clord was about to pick up. And Earth didn't seem quite so distant anymore.

CATABILID CONQUEST

You would never believe it, but our greatest adventure actually began one day a couple of months ago as Vana, my twin, and I sat under a tree, wallowing in absolute misery.

"Vana," I said, "what are we going to do? We'd counted on their coming now." Neither one of us could understand why our parents had decided not to come home. They'd been gone for months. It just wasn't fair.

Vana looked at me, at a loss for words for the first time I could ever remember. "I don't know," he said finally. "There doesn't seem to be any way out for us. We ought to go on our sequestering in the next three or four weeks, if we're going to have any choice at all in what we do at school next year. I don't think I can stand another year of that standard course."

"Almost everyone else is gone," I added.

Vana nodded and didn't reply. We both knew the fix we were in. We live with our grandparents because our parents own and fly a small spaceship, one that delivers supplies to archaeological digs on other planets. As a result, they are seldom home.

We had always liked the freedom this gave us. Our

grandparents both teach at the Master Level School and are deep into subjects that have to do with hidden areas of the mind: Earth Power and what it can do. So unless we did something that really called attention to ourselves, we could pretty much do as we pleased.

This had all worked very well until it came time for us to go on a sequestering. Everyone has to go on one in order to move from the standard course in school to one that meets one's own interests and talents. On a sequestering you pull yourself together and find out who you are and what you want of the future. But adults, and especially parents, have to be a part of it.

Our grandparents couldn't understand our need for a sequestering. "It's an old-fashioned concept," they said. "You children are secure enough. And in the end all education must come from within you."

At school, everyone said it had to be parents who were involved anyway. "Wait until your parents come home," we were told again and again.

The real trouble, we had decided, was that we simply didn't fit into any pattern that anyone else considered normal, and no one knew what to do with us. Even our grandparents sometimes seemed a little embarrassed by us. Earth people don't have many children. Twins are something no one knows anything about. And to make it worse, most people don't think it's wise to leave Earth unless they really have to. Archaeologists leave, and government people, to work in other places for a while. But to choose to be gone almost all the time—well, that's just not normal. So by being twins and by having parents who are always away, by choice, we had become outsiders. We had hoped that a sequestering would prove that we really were like other people and deserved a place to belong.

We sat under the tree in silence, going over and over our problem. Only the really stupid kids, the ones who had no choice about their futures, would be left in the standard school next year. And we had been bored this year. We had counted on the promised three-week visit from our parents. Surely they would listen, we felt, would understand, would care, would arrange things. But now they weren't coming. Instead they were taking emergency equipment off to some weird place called Frod, where a small dig was taking place. A number of different planets were participating, but this particular gear only Earth could supply. Earth is big on archaeology because of its history. Its archaeologists are called in on special projects in lots of places, even by planets that are more developed.

"We've got to do something," I said at last. "Think of something, Vana."

"Think of something yourself," he muttered.

I did have an idea in the back of my mind, but I hadn't wanted to say anything for fear he would laugh. We had to find some answer, though. So I blurted it out.

"Well, why don't we plan our own sequestering? If we went away, and kept careful notes to show people, maybe that would be enough. There wouldn't be the rituals at the start and end, but we could show we have some ability anyway. Getting away would prove that."

Vana looked at me with amazement. He always thinks boys should be the ones with ideas. "That might just work," he said. "It just might." His whole face brightened.

"Look," he went on, "no one would miss us, at least not at first, if we planned right. We could go far enough away so no one would think to look for us where we were, then come back after three or four days. It would be great. If nothing else, it would be something different to do, and we sure need that."

"There's no place we can walk to where no one would look for us," I said, a little annoyed that he had taken over my idea so completely. "In fact, I can't think of any place we could get to that someone wouldn't look, except maybe Frod." Frod was simply the farthest away place I could think of at the moment. But then suddenly. . . .

An electric spark jumped between us, and we both grinned. We knew we both had the same idea. It was so obvious. Why had it taken us so long to think of? We could go to Frod. Our sequestering would be a stolen trip to Frod! It was the greatest idea we had ever had.

"It would work," Vana said, almost breathless. "We could do it. I know we could." And thinking it over, I agreed. Together we could make it happen.

According to the report we had received, our parents were expected at the space port they used in just a week. They would arrive late one evening and leave early the next morning. They were bringing in only a few things that would have to be unloaded, and only a few new things would have to be loaded for the trip to Frod. We would have one night in which to get aboard the spaceship and find places to hide.

We had visited the space port and the spaceship

several times in the past. We knew of places at the space port where we could wait unseen, and we could think of several places in the ship that would probably be empty on the trip to Frod.

Almost before we knew it, our plans were roaring along and were almost completed. We tried to nail down every detail of our going. And the more we planned, the more confident we became.

We told our grandparents that a message had come from the space port saying that our parents had asked us to come for a short visit while they were in. It sounded logical because they had been gone so long. Our grandparents believed us. They had no reason not to.

Our next chore was to gather condensed food and the kinds of liquids that you only need a little of to keep from being thirsty. That was harder, but we managed. We both had some money, and we found ways to buy quietly and in small bits.

The hardest part was to keep the excitement out of our voices and faces. That was the thing that would give us away, if anything did. We didn't wholly succeed, but luckily no one noticed.

When the time came for us to leave, we were all ready. We set off with more gear than anyone should have thought necessary for a brief trip to a space port. But no one asked any awkward questions. We took the Mechanized Transport, which was very safe. People mind their own business on the Transport.

The base was just as we remembered it. We found a place to hide, and saw our parents' ship come down just after sundown. We watched them get off, obviously tired and ready to sleep. Good, there was no danger of their taking time to call us or our grandparents.

A gang of workers took a few things from the ship and put a few more things on. The steps to the cabin were left in place, and the door was left open because the ship was leaving so early in the morning. Other workers, on the far side of the ship, would be refueling it all night, so obviously no one thought there was any danger in leaving things open.

Under cover of dark, and the scant vegetation of the desert area where the space port was, we crept to the ship, slipped up the stairs, and were in. It was almost too easy.

We had remembered two special closets, generally used for fragile artifacts, that we were sure would be available to us. It was dark in the ship, with only a few landing lights on, but we found the closets after a short search and crept in. We felt very safe in our hideaways. Only in emergencies were they used for supplies. And like most of the ship, they had oxygen outlets.

The next day the ship took off. We were a bit shaken up by the blast-off, but our closets were padded, so we weren't hurt. We had made it into space! I felt like cheering as soon as I came out of my blackout. Now, even when our grandparents discovered we were gone, which wasn't likely for another day or two, no one could do a thing. No one was likely to guess where we were. And we would have our sequestering.

We had been in our closets for almost twenty-four earth hours when Vana called me.

"What are we going to do now?" I asked, coming out.

"Stretch," Vana said.

"And then what?"

"Plot our course," he muttered.

"It's plotted for us," I said. "We're going to Frod."

"Don't be stupid. The question is, what do we do when we get there? And how do we get back if these closets are filled for the return?"

I looked at him in amazement. I hadn't thought of that. But I was sure he had. He's generally so thorough.

"I was busy planning how to get away, of course," he said, to my unspoken question. "Coming back wasn't important until we left."

"What are the options?" I asked.

"Do we want to be found?" he said.

At first it seemed a silly question, then it didn't. If we were found it would solve some of our problems, problems that now seemed all too obvious, although we had both evidently overlooked them before. Yet being found would create other problems that could be much worse. We wouldn't have to worry about food and getting home. But we would have to worry about a scolding or more—the Guardians only know what— and about being watched too closely, maybe forever. Certainly if we were found before we got to Frod, we wouldn't see much of that planet.

"I say no," I answered at last.

"Me too," said Vana. "If we can make it. It all depends on Frod. And on what they pick up there."

We had done some research on Frod, but hadn't been able to find out much about it. It wasn't a large planet, but it was quite heavy, so gravity was close to Earth's. It had once had intelligent life, but that life now seemed gone. Archaeologists were trying to find out what had happened. Why, we didn't know, because as far as we had been able to discover there had never been the kind of life that would make such research worthwhile. Yet it must have been important if Earth archaeologists were there. They only go out when they're really needed. People on other planets still feel a little strange about being with Earth people.

"We won't have enough food if we can't get some there," I said.

"Or water," Vana said. "Of course, in an emergency we can get it from the ship's tanks, but we can hardly do that often without someone's noticing."

"I'll fix that," I said.

"How?" Vana asked.

"Put in a few pebbles each time, to keep the level up."

"You don't have any pebbles."

"I can get some on Frod." I couldn't imagine a planet without stones of some kind.

He let that pass, not having a better suggestion.

"Can we stand a week in these closets? Maybe a week each way?" I asked, stretching my stiff muscles again.

"We have to. We chose it," Vana said.

I grinned wryly. He was right, we had.

So we both stretched some more and didn't talk. There was nothing more to say. We had made all the plans we could. The rest depended on Frod.

It seems a miracle that we were not discovered on that trip out. The spaceship was compact. There was little room that wasn't filled with something. And we did move around a bit in our compartments. We must have made some noise in our sleep, when our parents were awake. But I guess the idea of stowaways had never occurred to them, so they just didn't hear the noises.

It was a sequestering, all right. Sleeping was hard. We were so tired sometimes, we could have slept standing up in broad daylight. But after only a little sleep huddled in those closets, we woke up feeling cramped again. There wasn't much time, we found, when we could be out of our nests. One or the other of our parents was generally awake. A short trip takes more navigation than a longer one. You pass through time bumps more often.

I got a bit of thinking done, and Vana did too. Part of it was about our problem. What we would do on Frod. Food. Water. We rationed what we had brought carefully to last the trip out, so these things became more and more important. You always think about what you can't have, I guess. At least you do if you want it.

I discovered a few things about myself. I like people and I like new things and new ideas. And suddenly I didn't blame our parents for the life they led. I decided that given a chance I'd do the same myself. Vana, I discovered later, came to the same decision on that outward trip. Maybe it was mental telepathy. Don't laugh. Some places have it. And our Earth Power is not so different. Since one is supposed to develop one's powers on a sequestering, maybe ours were moving in new directions because we were going on a new kind of sequestering. Actually, we both knew how to focus, which is why our grandparents hadn't worried and said we were secure.

The time went by slowly. It was hard to keep track of days. But eventually we felt the ship enter a new phase. There was a change of power, and a sense of direction to what we were doing. We were nearing Frod.

Vana and I held fast in our closets, afraid the landing would jar us out of our senses. But, although we were tossed around a bit, it wasn't as bad as blast-off. Worst of all was a gradual clamping at us, a feeling of heaviness that we could hardly bear. There was a sharp smack, a swaying, and we were down. It was strange to be still, and stranger still to feel the gravity of Frod.

We heard all sorts of things going on almost at once. Obviously someone had been waiting for the ship. We were really quiet then, listening to the sounds of unloading. Someone nearly opened my door, but I held it shut, and whoever it was thought it was locked. A strange voice said something I didn't understand, and the person at the door went away.

Eventually it was quiet, but I waited until Vana called before I crept out. He was on the door side and could hear what was going on there better than I. It was dark in the ship, but I could tell that all the stuff had been unloaded.

"Let's go," Vana whispered. "Take all your gear."

We crept down the passageway, alert, waiting for any breath of sound. None came. So far so good. No one around inside . The door to the outside was at the left. Closed? Locked? I tried it softly, quietly. No! Not locked.

"Not all the way," Vana murmured at me.

I shook my head and shoved the door open a crack. There was no sound. Another crack. Still no sound. And now I could see that stairs outside led to the ground. Fortunately it was night on Frod. No one would see us, I hoped. I slid through the crack and went down the steps. Vana followed, carefully closing the door behind him. Again, everything seemed almost too easy. We were on Frod. We had done what we had planned to do.

We lay flat on the soil of Frod, hidden by the stairs and the spaceship from any eyes that might be near. In the distance we saw someone, a watchman, perhaps. But there was no sign that he had seen us.

Sliding on our stomachs, we moved slowly over the dark ground, our packs on our backs. It seemed most important that we not be discovered. We had come to see Frod, and now we were going to see it. By ourselves. We moved away from the watchman and the one building in the distance. Which meant we were also moving away from any signs of habitation and gliding toward a forest where the plants looked something like tropical plants on Earth. Broad heavy leaves. Some small. Some large. The whole was so dense we wondered if we could force ourselves into the protection of it.

Because we had to, we managed. By the time the moon of Frod came up, huge and brilliant, we were sitting under and surrounded by the oddest plants we had ever seen. They were strong and thick and seemed to grow while we watched.

"Whew!" said Vana. "Here we are, and now what?"

"I thought you were working that out," I said.

"Couldn't till we got here to see what it was like."

"How long have we got?"

"That I do know. They're due back at sunset on the twenty-fifth of Westerg. We left on the fourth. This is the eleventh, I think. If it takes as long to get back as it did to come, we've got seven days, or six days, if we want to play it safe."

I did. "Six days then," I said. "Six days to find food and water and a place on the ship to hide."

"I thought we came for a sequestering," Vana said, laughing.

"I've had it," I said. "Seven days on the way out. And if we're lucky, seven days on the way back. That's enough. Besides, to find food and water, we have to explore. And I'd rather do that. If we can get through all this greenery, that is." As I spoke, I felt doubtful and must have sounded it. It was such an odd place.

"Frod is different," Vana admitted. "I didn't think it would be like this."

We both looked around carefully. The field where we had landed seemed to be cut out of a solid bed of growth. It was like an oasis in the middle of a terrarium gone wild. At least as far as we could see. Which wasn't all that far.

"We've got a little food," Vana said. "So we don't have to worry right away about how much of this is edible. Why don't we sleep until it's light. Things may look better then."

The Frodian night was not as dark as ours. In addition to the moon, something in the atmosphere seemed to glow. But no light would have been enough to keep us awake. It felt too good to stretch out on the ground.

We woke to a Frodian day that turned out to be not quite so bright as ours on Earth. It seemed strange after that bright night sky. Whatever made the sky glow at night seemed to hold out some of the rays of Frod's star in the day. It still was bright enough, considering we had seen very little light in almost eight days. We both blinked as we woke.

"Forgot my dark glasses," Vana said.

I laughed. It seemed such a normal thing to forget. "What else do you need?" I asked.

"Food first," he said.

So it was food first. Our careful ration. And a little water. Then we looked around. There wasn't much to see that we hadn't already seen. Plants everywhere. Light green. Medium green. Dark green. Yellow green, blue green, all shades of green. And all succulents of a sort. Yet not desert plants. Lush, the products of a rain forest, and dense. The soil had to be very rich to support such growth, I thought. But even given that, the growth seemed overmuch.

"If we go far into this, how will we know where we are?" I said. "We may never find the field again. Do you have a compass?"

"Silly!" Vana thought he was being smart. "We have no idea of where the magnetic poles are here, or even if there are any."

"Well, if there is one, does it matter where it is, as long as we know what direction we're moving in?" I asked.

Vana looked at me in surprise. "You're right," he said. "And I think I do have a compass. Left from that last hiking trip." He searched in his bag and pulled out a tiny compass. The needle swung to a fixed position, so the place did have a magnetic pole of some sort.

We set out in the direction the compass pointed, which happened to be parallel to the field. It was hard going. Some of the plants had sharp edges. The ones near the ground obviously needed little light because they flourished under a canopy of heavy leaves made by the tree-like plants. And in between there was a bush level. It was almost dark on the ground.

We moved on for an hour or an hour and a half.

"How long is a day here?" I asked.

"About twenty of our hours," Vana answered.

"Will the ship be here six or seven of our days or theirs?"

Vana just shrugged his shoulders. He had no way of knowing. So we had less time on Frod than I had thought. We'd have to be back in six Frodian days. Or maybe be left behind. And the job of finding what we needed looked bigger every minute. We saw no water and didn't know what was edible among these plants.

We plodded on, or rather pushed and pressed our way—silently. We had no idea where we were going or what we hoped to find. We were alone on a strange planet, and no one knew we were there. Yet not for a minute did we want to be found. It was still an adventure.

"Where do you suppose the archaeological team is working?" Vana asked as we slowed to rest.

"How can they find anything at all in this?" I asked. "What ever made them think there was intelligent life here once?"

"I think they must be on the other side of the clearing," he said. "That's where the building was. The dig or whatever it is must be near the clearing. You couldn't carry supplies very far in this. Of course," he added, "it may not all be like this."

"Do we try to find the dig?" I asked.

"I don't know. We don't want to be found. But food and water may be easier to find there." It was the first time I had ever heard Vana be really uncertain. And suddenly the six Frodian days seemed long, longer than six Earth days. Especially if we had to spend them near some stupid dig with an uncertain future at the end.

"We've been walking inside the forest but parallel to the field," Vana said at last. "If we make a sharp right, we should go over the top of the field—somewhat beyond it, I expect. Let's walk a hundred or a hundred and fifty paces to the right and see what we come to."

We moved slowly to the right, but the scenery remained the same. The field was not there. The compass said we were doing what we had planned. We had been going due north by the compass. And now we were headed due east, or as near to it as we could manage with all the stuff growing in our way.

"Shall we go back south a way?" I asked.

We did and still saw no open space. Yet we had moved so slowly through the heavy growth we couldn't have come too far beyond it.

"Is there really a magnetic pole here?" I asked timidly.

"You and your fancy ideas!" Vana sank to the ground. And I settled heavily beside him. The compass needle seemed true. But was it? Where were we?

And where was the spaceship? I began to be afraid for the first time.

"We could follow our trail back," I said.

We both looked in the direction we thought we had come. Nothing. All around. Nothing. We had pushed through and left no trail. But how was that possible, especially when we had sometimes broken off the stiff leaves as we came along? Why were there no signs of our passage anywhere?

"Where are we?" I whispered.

"You are on his majesty's planet Cheriba," a voice answered.

It was a pleasant voice. But that didn't keep it from being electrifying, even terrifying.

Vana and I looked at each other. Frod was uninhabited, except for plants. And no archaeologist would have said a thing like that. Had our spaceship made an unscheduled landing? I had never heard of Cheriba.

Vana looked shaken. We moved closer together and glanced around. There was no one anywhere. We looked up at the high plants. They covered the sky. We couldn't have seen the ship if it had left. But it was scheduled only for Frod. And the supplies had been taken off. This must be Frod!

"Here, under the bush," the voice said.

We hardly dared to look. But there under the bush was a little brown lump. A cross between a stone and a turtle shell. Nothing that looked alive. Certainly nothing that could talk. Yet as I watched, the whole thing rose, hovered in the air a moment, and then slowly moved toward us. It was an amazing sight. I drew back, ready to stand and run if necessary. Vana, I could feel, was as tense as I.

"You don't look like the others. Earth, aren't you? But smaller," said the voice from the turtle-rock, as it settled before us.

Neither of us replied.

"No matter. The question is, what's to be done with you? None of the others were foolish enough, or venturesome enough, to wander off. You really aren't lost, you know. You just came too far. As others of you have discovered, directions aren't easy here for those who don't know the place. Your noisy airfield is over there." The creature hopped a little back and to the right. We nodded and remained still.

"I'm not sure I can let you go there, though. You may not be like the rest. But this may have been planned. Can't be sure. Can't take a chance. Yet you seemed less certain than the others. More friendly, and really lost. I felt sorry. . . ." Its voice trailed off into nothing, as if it were thinking deeply.

"But we don't want to go back. At least not right away. If this really is Frod," I ventured. The thing sounded so friendly I felt I had to take a chance.

The creature said nothing for a moment.

"This is what they call Frod," it said finally. "But it really is Cheriba."

"But Frod is uninhabited," I said, "except for plants. At least that's what the archaeologists think."

"There are some who think this planet is uninhabited," said the creature with dignity. "We who live here think otherwise. However, we are not eager that those who have come should discover our presence."

"I guess not," said Vana. "Not if they're here to dig

up a dead civilization. You might complicate things. And besides, you can't tell what they might do with you. Can you protect yourselves?"

"We have our ways," our turtle-rock said slyly. "And as for dead civilizations, that's absurd." The creature seemed to chuckle. "I shouldn't be telling you this, though. There are those of us who will never trust outlings. And that is what you are."

"We are, and we aren't, " Vana muttered.

"Why do you talk like us, if you're from here?" I asked, before the creature could say any more.

"Learned from those digging fools." Our companion chuckled again. "They're digging up our garbage pile, and they don't even know we're here." With that, our friend rolled over and over in the underbrush, howling with laughter. We were so amazed we simply sat and watched until there was another question.

"You're with the Earth bunch?"

I looked at Vana, and he looked at me.

"Not really," I began slowly. "We're more like you. Unseen." And then, hardly realizing what I was doing, I told our whole story, all of it.

When I finished, our turtle-rock gave a quick snort.

"Serves them right," it muttered. "No sense. None at all. Looking into other people's garbage."

"Are you all like you?" Vana asked.

"Of course. Always have been. No reason to change. Very comfortable shape. And especially good these days. They think we're stones. Now, how long did you say you have?"

I told it what we had figured. Six Frodian days—Cheriban days.

"Good," it said. "Plenty of time. Come with me."

And it set off with its queer flying jumps that seemed to have no means of propulsion behind them whatsoever.

I looked at Vana and he looked at me, and we followed. It was the airfield or our new friend. And our new friend seemed to offer the best chance for adventure. Though what else we might be getting into, we didn't even dare guess.

"Why don't they realize about you?" I asked finally.

"Because they've got no sense," our friend said quickly. Then it added, "Though, of course, we don't give them much chance." It chuckled again, but didn't go on.

Vana and I found the going hard. The undergrowth, which had seemed dense before, grew denser. Our friend flew over the lower plants in high hops. But we couldn't. Still we went on, and after a bit I began to feel good about it all, even though I was getting very tired.

"Whew!" Vana said finally. "We can't move as fast as you. By the way, do you have a name? My name is Vana, and this is my sister, Chory."

Our friend stopped, and if an almost-rock can bow, it did. "Honored," it said. "Not every creature gives its name so easily. I'm Quelot. And I forgot that you Earthlings have never learned to bounce. Do you want to learn? It'll be easier for you to get around here, even at your size."

Quelot spoke as if we might take our choice. But who wouldn't want to! Although I didn't for a minute believe I could. Vana nodded his head, yet I could tell he was dubious, too.

"We'd love to, Mister Quelot," he said.

"Not 'Mister,' just Quelot. No fanciness here. All alike."

We nodded. Then Quelot seemed to ponder a moment.

"You creatures from Earth, you have a great power. Not like most who come. You should find this easy. I wouldn't try otherwise. Can you do the Earth-Power thing?"

We nodded. We could focus. It was a useful thing, focusing, though not so all-powerful as some minded planets might think.

"It's not so different from that, I guess. Same sort of concentration. Just use the pressure in another way. Instead of holding things still, just push the ground away."

It sounded easy, but it wasn't as simple as it sounded. I pushed and pushed and nothing happened. Vana looked finally as if he were about to explode. And still he didn't move. I suppose I looked just as silly.

Quelot looked on patiently, seemingly convinced we would master it before long. We were not so sure.

We tried some more.

Still nothing.

"Not with part of you," Quelot said finally. "All of you, and don't force it. Relax and pressure down. I forgot that you sometimes use tension to trigger your power. That doesn't work with this."

I stopped a moment, worn out with trying. Vana, I could see, was working to relax and still getting nowhere.

Finally I pulled myself together and gave it another

go. Maybe it was because I had almost given up. Maybe it was because I had really relaxed for a moment. Or maybe it was because I accidentally found the key to how to place the pressure. But suddenly I rose about a decimeter into the air. It was the strangest thing that had ever happened to me. And I must have looked as surprised as I felt because Quelot was once more off into that wild, happy hysteria we had seen before. I let go and settled to the ground, but before I said anything, I did it again, this time propelling myself just a bit higher and a little forward.

"How . . .?" Vana began, looking at me in amazement. And at that moment he too rose into the air. We had both done it. And the most astonishing thing was that it was easy, once you felt how.

"Will this work at home?" Vana asked.

"Of course," said Quelot. "If you need it there. You have all kinds of machines."

"Not so many on Earth," I said. "We're not big machine people."

Quelot bobbled in surprise. "I thought you outlings were all alike underneath."

"Oh, no," Vana cried. "You might even like Earth. You wouldn't like Clord or Campion or Gammer. At least not from what I've heard. I've never been there. But Earth has a lot of peace on it."

"I'm content with Cheriba," Quelot said.

"You sound like most Earth people," Vana said.

Quelot made no reply, just went hopping off, and we followed. It was obvious at once that it was a lot easier to bounce than to walk over and through the vegetation.

We went on for what seemed hours, with no idea of

where we were going. I began to worry, and I saw a questioning look on Vana's face too. We were hungry and tired, and we didn't know where we were. Neither of us said anything. But Quelot must have sensed our mood.

"Nearly there," our guide said, stopping a moment. "Are you hungry? I've noticed that outlings eat a lot."

We nodded. "It's time to eat," I ventured.

"Can you wait a bit?"

We nodded again. And once more we bounced off.

"Are we going to see the king?" Vana asked tentatively.

That set Quelot off once more. Our new friend was the jolliest creature I had ever encountered. Earth people laugh sometimes. But not like that. Quelot seemed to find laughter in everything.

"Oh, my," our turtle-rock mumbled at last. "I'd almost forgotten. His majesty's planet Cheriba! Of course you believed it. But I was just being like an outling. I didn't know you then. There's no king. We all just live. Well, it's not quite that simple, but you'll see. Just don't expect a king."

So we didn't expect a king, or an emperor, or a Commander of All the Cheribas. Or even a Core Council. But what were we to expect?

We bounced along in silence. If we hadn't left any trail pushing and shoving our way through the lush growth, we were leaving less of one now, bouncing from spot to spot. We were totally dependent on Quelot and others of Cheriba, if we ever got to them. If they were all as friendly and helpful as Quelot seemed, we were fine. But if not and we were left alone in the jungle, we were going to be very lost.

into what, all at once, seemed the most marvelous place in the galaxy.

I was so full of glee that at first I didn't even realize anyone else was there. But when I bumped into a rolling rock, I knew that Vana and I weren't the only ones howling with laughter and spinning in delight. The clearing was alive with friends of Quelot and Turstive. It was almost like a ceremony, a convention, a demonstration, or maybe a dance, with everyone taking an active part.

I didn't want it to stop, but quite suddenly it did. And I stopped with everyone else. Vana did too.

"Oh, my!" said one of our friends. "That was the best ever. Quelot, where did you find them?"

"Lost," another rock-like creature said, Quelot obviously, though we hadn't yet learned to tell one from another. Our friend summarized the whole story.

"Allies?" another rock asked.

"Oh, yes," Quelot said.

Then before we knew what was happening, we were surrounded by dense circles of rocks, all of them the living creatures of Cheriba. We were surrounded, but not frightened.

"Who and what are you?" Vana asked.

"We are Catabilids, or so we call ourselves," said one, stepping out of the inner circle and up to us. "We live in these forests of Cheriba, and the Daphamaris live in the more open places. You could not tell the difference between us, the Catabilids and the Daphamaris, but we know ourselves. Yet we are friends. And together we cultivate and enjoy our place in the galaxy."

115

"How do you talk? Have you hands or feet?" I asked.

"Mostly mind we are, covered with a hard outer protection. We bounce, as you have seen. And we have several small openings through which we absorb certain chemicals that are our foods, and through which we can project sounds made by certain of our organs within. We also have a couple of things you might call hands." He put out a stringy sort of appendage at an odd angle, with two fingers and a thumb at the end. "We have a language of our own. But we have been able to learn yours and those of the others quite quickly."

"And where do you live?" I asked. "I mean, do you have houses?"

"Most certainly," said the spokesman. "We have holes in some of our larger plants. Very comfortable. Not your size, of course. But good for us, and full of the sorts of things that make us happy. Now, how much time do you have?"

"Five days after this, we think," Vana said.

"Five days, then," said the speaker. "And by the way, my name is Ganid. I am the current leader of the Catabilids in this area. Quelot and Turstive are two of my assistants. Although we really don't have governments as you do. No need, really. Ours is a simple life."

"Let's get on," said a voice I recognized as Turstive's. "Five days. Time enough."

For what, I wondered.

A snicker, that was all I could call it, passed through the ranks of Catabilids.

"What do you want of us?" Vana asked, suddenly alarmed.

"To help us convince the outlings they should leave," said Ganid.

"But we can't do that!" Vana said. "They would never listen to us."

"Didn't say they would," Quelot spoke up. "We have our ways, but we could use some help."

"You're not going to hurt them?" I asked hesitantly.

"No need," said Quelot.

"Let me explain," said Ganid. "We Catabilids farm the forest. The plants are our friends, so to speak. They provide us with the chemicals we need, and we in turn provide them with what they need. The growth in this area is a bit heavier than we really like it, except right here; but it's all planned. As I'm sure you realize, growth is a protection for us. Those fool diggers have tried everything, chemicals from every planet, to stop the growth, and nothing works. Because we neutralize what they bring, and put down the things that will make our plants grow. That airfield, for example, is a real problem to them. Ten of them spend all day every day keeping it cut. And it grows faster than they can work. The dig site—where they're finding our old stools and other things we make to have around, all worn out, of course—is overgrown every morning. They spend half of every day cutting plants. A little more growth, and they'll all go home. But the chemicals we use we make ourselves, mostly, inside us, and we're using all we can make. The next complex of Catabilids would give us some of theirs. Any complex anywhere would, for that matter.

It's to everyone's good that we get rid of these out-lings. But each group is needed where it is. Can't leave for long. And as you can see, we can't carry much. So we have trouble bringing in the extra sup-plies we need. But you can do it. You're big, and you have big hands."

The idea was clear at once. And I loved it. Those diggers had no right to be here, really. Even our par-ents were interlopers. The Catabilids had first rights. People could dig up their own past. But why explore someone else's garbage heap? The outlings were just being nosy. More to the point, someone from some overcrowded planet probably wanted to settle here and wanted to be sure it was safe before a ship and colo-nists were sent in. The idea made me shudder.

"I'm with you," Vana said.

"When do we start?" I asked.

"It's nearly dark now." It was Quelot again. "Morn-ing is time enough. We'll bring food then. Do you need water?"

We said yes.

"Fine. Why don't you sleep now? Right here will be fine. It should be warm enough for you."

In an amazing surge, the Catabilids all bounded off. I wanted to talk to Vana, but I was too sleepy. I didn't even eat. I just fell asleep.

The morning light slid obliquely through the tall plants as I awoke, only vaguely aware of someone be-side me. It was a Catabilid. Another was waking Vana.

"Time to be up." My Catabilid was Quelot. The other was Turstive. "But here, eat." Quelot pointed to specific leaves. I took one and found it wasn't tough, but rather solid and quite sweet. Another had a rather melony texture and a spicy taste.

"Good," I said.

"Cheriba has everything," Quelot said.

Vana, meanwhile, was getting the same treatment from Turstive.

"There's water on the way," Quelot told me. "Better get started, to be there and back before night."

We bounced off through the forest at a faster pace than the day before. But we seemed to have no trouble, Vana and I. We didn't even get tired. No one said much. Yet I knew Vana was pleased with our project, and so was I.

We moved through the forest for several hours, stopping now and then at small pools for water and a carefully pointed-out leaf or bud. Our guides seemed to know just what plants we should have. I wondered if some were poisonous, but didn't ask. It didn't matter, so long as we had friends.

Finally we came to a rather new kind of vegetation, less dark, less dense.

"New territory," Quelot said.

Vana and I nodded, not really understanding.

"Here they come," said Turstive.

And there they did come. A whole flying army of Catabilids. I wondered why they didn't just fly at the diggers. That should scare them away, certainly. But then I realized that once the Catabilids had let themselves be discovered, they would be hunted down and carried all over our part of the galaxy, as a curiosity. Which would be a shame. They loved their planet so, and they were happy here.

There was a conference in their own language. Obviously only the Catabilids in the invaded area had become linguists. Then we all went over to what seemed to be a log hollowed out from one end and filled with a sweet-smelling liquid. That was what we were to carry. But how could we do it and not spill anything, bouncing along as we must.

Quelot sensed our question and said, "We'll put a heavy leaf on top. That should do it."

And in a few minutes it was ready. A tough leathery leaf had been fastened to the stump with sticky stuff from another plant. The plants of Cheriba did seem to provide everything. On request? Maybe so, since they were considered friends.

The leaf cover was strong enough that we could turn the log end for end and carry it between us. It took a while for Vana and I to coordinate our bounces, but after a few tries, we did pretty well. The return trip took longer, though. It was nearly dark when we arrived back at our clearing.

"Good, just what we need for tonight," Ganid greeted us. "But you are tired. We have water here for you in small containers and some leaves." We looked gratefully at small cups made of thick stems, full of water, and a pile of leaves. It had not been easy for our friends to gather so much and bring it all to the clearing. The Catabilids had very small "hands." They were obviously a thoughtful people.

"Thank you," Vana said.

"You are really kind," I added.

"No, it is you who are kind. Or perhaps we are helping each other, as we and our plants do," Ganid said.

We ate and fell asleep at once.

Morning came in the same way it had the day before. But it was not quite so light.

"Early," said Quelot, confirming my observation. "We thought you'd like to see what we've done. Lots of plants at the dig."

Vana and I were up in a moment, bouncing after Quelot and Turstive. We had not seen the dig before; and we soon discovered that we weren't really going to see it then. Bush-size plants were growing all over it. From a place well hidden, we saw people of several outling varieties looking dazed. And then we realized that not only had the bushes grown more than usual overnight, but the tree trunks that ringed the dig site had become so much thicker that the three small tractors the diggers had used could not get out. They sat there trapped.

I giggled.

"Sh!" Quelot warned. "See the field."

We nodded.

The field beyond was more of the same. The spaceship was surrounded by bushes. There were tractors there, too, but even with them that field wasn't going to get cleared in one day.

"One night, maybe two more," said Turstive with a chuckle.

"What if our parents leave before they planned?" I asked.

"We will know. You won't be left. You'll have food and water too," Quelot said.

How it would all be managed, we didn't know. But we trusted the Catabilids. They seemed amazingly competent.

That day and the next were repetitions of the first,

except that we went to different places, each about the same distance as the first.

The morning after the third night of extra feeding, the whole outling camp was in a state of alarm. The tractors were totally useless, all hemmed in. In fact, some of the heavier members of the digging party had to pass sideways between the taller, thicker plants when they went to the dig site. They might just as well not have gone. The dig was obliterated. The diggers could only stand and stare. Yet all of them were there. Our parents too, as confused as the rest. I wondered what they would think if they knew. It seemed best, somehow, that they not find out. I wondered if the Catabilids thought that too.

"What if our parents go home early?" I asked again.

"Won't happen," Quelot murmured. "Strange winds in those buildings. All loose things held down with Catabilids."

For a minute I could hardly hold in my laughter. A perfect spy system. Quelot shook with inner laughter too. We backed away quietly. And Vana followed.

"What's wrong with you two?" he asked.

I explained. He howled aloud before he remembered where we were. Quelot hastily beckoned for us to move more quickly, and we did. Then back in the clearing we laughed until we thought we'd shake apart. Only when we were so weak we couldn't laugh anymore did we really begin to cope with the problem of getting home.

"Do you think," Turstive asked, "that you could make one more trip, a short one this time? Only half a day. Just in case. And we'll keep watch and have everything ready. We won't let them go without you. And you needn't worry about food and water or even quarters for your trip. We'll take care of that."

We could only agree. We couldn't solve our problems for ourselves. And so far the Catabilids had done well for us, and, of course, we had helped them a lot in return. So we went to a nearer group of Catabilids where we got another log full of growing juice. I wondered what would happen if I tasted some, but decided it was better not to know.

We got back in the middle of the Cheriban afternoon, and Ganid was there to greet us.

"Glad to see you!" the leader exclaimed loudly. "The results of your work have certainly been better than even we anticipated." Only remarkable self-restraint seemed to keep Ganid from rolling into a great spasm of laughter. "Spaceships have been called for everyone. Dangerous planet, they say. Too small to bother with. Wild growth of no use, even for animal food. Your parents are leaving in the morning with the most important Earth diggers."

"And what about us?" I asked, afraid once again. Now the ship would really be full. I was sure we'd be found. And that would ruin everything.

"No problem," said Ganid. "There are a number of crates being loaded now, in the pressurized cargo area. Two of them hold samples of Cheriban plant life, of obvious interest to scientists everywhere. These are not solidly packed. And they are not air-tight. One of you in each, with several containers of water, will work quite well. We have seen to it that all the plants in each box are edible and useful to you."

"But won't they wonder about its all being gone if we eat it?"

"Who knows what happens to Cheriban plant stuffs when they come into an alien atmosphere? They may just go *poof!* Certainly we Catabilids could not exist elsewhere." Ganid did begin to laugh then.

It would be the final joke. Vana and I looked at each other and roared until we remembered it meant leaving. Then the joke almost seemed to be on us.

That night the Catabilids helped us into the proper boxes. They had even seen to it that the boxes were placed on top of the other cargo so we could get in and out easily. We had no trouble getting to the ship without being seen because by that time the new growth was so high even a giant would have been hidden. A narrow trail was kept open from the camp building, but otherwise the field was completely overgrown. There were no guards. None of the outlings would stay apart from the others. They were afraid they'd be lost forever. So we moved in easily, settled down, and waited for morning.

The parting with the Catabilids went quickly. None of us could say what we felt. I really wished I could stay, and Vana did too. But we couldn't. We belonged on Cheriba no more than the diggers did. The Catabilids had a right to keep their planet for themselves, and to live as they chose to live.

The next morning the Earthlings came out—our parents and two men and a woman. They carried small bags. The rest of their gear had obviously been stowed earlier.

"Do you think you can lift off?" one of the men said in a worried tone.

"Positive," said my father. "Strangest things I've

ever seen, these plants. But we've taken off from worse places."

The man grunted. No one else spoke. And in a few minutes we felt the now almost familiar swift rise. We were facing seven days in our crates, Vana and I. Although we might find moments when we could crawl out, obviously they would be few. Still, we had a lot to think about. And surely there would be some moments to move and stretch.

We needed to move about less than we had thought we would. The plants seemed to keep us in a state where a lot of movement was unnecessary. All of our bodily functions were slowed down. Yet, except when I slept, my mind was clear.

In those hours we had our real sequestering. But we did not find what others usually found. I discovered that the nicest thing I had ever known was the laughter I had heard and experienced in Cheriba. It was gentle, even kind, and it came from true delight. That was what I wanted more than anything. That kind of laughter. And the life that went with it.

Vana said that he decided he wanted to explore in a spaceship, not to dig, but to find more unlikely places where he felt at home. I liked that idea too.

It was a strange goal for an Earthling. But I believed it was something to be jolly about. In fact in the few times we met out of our boxes, we were both very jolly. We recalled the things that had happened to us on Cheriba and felt again the delight we had known in being there.

"And just wait until we bounce on Earth!" Vana said.

We had agreed to get out of our boxes as soon as

possible on Earth, but not to be discovered near the space port, if possible. We hoped the ship would not be unloaded right away. Then we would have a chance to disappear before our empty boxes were found. Once out, we would move as far away as we could, then let ourselves be picked up. Somehow, it didn't matter what happened after that. We knew we'd be all right. We would say we'd gone on a sequestering ourselves, since no one would take us, and we'd gotten lost. That was, after all, sort of the truth of the matter.

We landed late in the day, as we had hoped we might. Whether or not the Catabilids had arranged that too, we didn't know, but they certainly had taken care of everything else. Just before coming down, we heard a loud exclamation and a rumble of voices that told us our parents had been informed of our absence. That was both good and bad, but mostly good. They'd be off in a hurry, looking for us. Even though we'd said we were coming to the base, no one would believe that, since no one had seen us.

In the excitement of landing and getting people out and away, we found plenty of chance to slip off. We wanted to stay and see what happened when those cases of greens turned out to be empty (we had the remaining leaves in our knapsacks), but even our new carefree state would not allow that. We hurried off into the night.

Two days later we were "found." We had spent the days wandering away from the field, following the Mechanized Transport lines as much as possible so as not to get completely lost. We had eaten up the plants

we had with us and used up our water. On our wan-
derings, we had spent a good deal of our time bouncing. It worked very well on Earth.

The second day we noticed a town in the distance,
and after getting our story straight between us, we
wandered in as if we had been lost a long time. In a
way we had been and still were; we had no idea of
what place we had come to.

At first the people in the town would not believe
us. But they sent our pictures to Central Com and discovered that we were the twins we said we were. Our
parents and a variety of officials arrived soon after.

They were all remarkably glad to see us. Vana and
I were both surprised. It was apparent that our parents did care, after all. We told our story: we hadn't
been allowed to go on a sequestering, so we had had
to go on our own and had gotten lost. We had lived on
plants. And we had discovered and learned all we
were supposed to learn and more. None of what we
said was false. We didn't even give any false impres-
sions. We just didn't tell everything.

They questioned us, of course. And when the questioning got a little tight, we brought up bouncing.
That finished the questions. We had to bounce over
and over. And everyone seemed as amazed at our not
being worn out by it as by our doing it at all.

Then we began to teach them. It was funny to see
adults try. Our father and mother got it very quickly,
and some others soon after. They looked so funny, we
had to laugh. We rolled on the ground with laughter,
but only we knew that we had learned bouncing and
laughing at the same time, from a Catabilid.

The next day they brought in a woman from the sequestering unit in the Central Core group; she also learned to bounce quickly. We liked her.

"Will you come and teach my leaders to bounce?" she asked.

"Sure, if we can," we said.

And we did.

People all over Earth, young and old, have learned to bounce now. But not many of them have learned to laugh as we do. Vana and I still roll with laughter, to the amazement of most people we know. Those plants we ate must have made us part Catabilid. I hope so.

The diggers are all gone from Cheriba, we've heard. The plants are a mystery still, both the ones on the planet and the missing ones we ate. We still hold to our dreams, though there is more of a place for us here on Earth than we had ever hoped there would be. We like it here, but we also hope to find new places where we will feel at home. Until then, Earth can be a good place. It is a good place, even if your parents fly a spaceship. Providing, of course, you find a way to go sequestering.

QUIET AND A WHITE BUSH

She woke slowly, almost as if she were pulling herself together, physically drawing herself in, letting herself become one again after she had been exploded into the diverse parts of her oneness. Where was she? That was the question to be settled first. She almost thought she knew. But then she knew she didn't. What she saw was like nothing she had seen before. The misty forms, the white rocks that were not real rocks, and the deep gray of the sky were not her world. But what world were they? And why?

She pushed a finger of thought into her mind and probed. Home? Yes, there was such a place. Earth. A comfortable bed? Yes, not just mushroom-like rocks that made hard pillows and knee rests and, if she wanted, places for sitting. Family? After a fashion. A mother and father and a brother. None of whom wholly understood her need for wildness, for distance. Aloneness was a part of them, but not apartness.

Where were they now? A hole. There had been a hole. In the place she had gone for quiet. An old stone quarry, left maybe from the pre-Clordian Sweep days. No one had ever checked. But the stones in the hole had been dark and in deep shadow. Not these queer white ones. And the sky there had been high and blue, not near and misty white.

Yet here she was. She rose on her side, propping herself on one elbow, and looked with deep concern at her surroundings. No one. A few growing things, also white. And the quiet. It was haunted, and yet it had a loveliness about it that she could not explain, even to herself. It was lonely too, and a bit frightening. What did one do here? Where did one go? Was the ground hard, like the rocks? No, it felt soft beneath her.

She rose unsteadily to her feet, drew herself up. She could stand. Her feet did not find the soil unyielding, but neither did they find it unsupporting. She took one step and then another. It was a tree, she suddenly realized, that stood above her. Strange, she hadn't noticed it. Or had it not been there before? Had it come because she suddenly perceived it? The thought made her mind reel. This was no time for guesses. It was a time to think wisely. The tree was there, and so was she. But what else? She sank to the rocks again.

She was reluctant to move from under the tree. The outer world seemed bare. Misty. Uncertain. If she left the tree, she might not find her way back. And the spot under the tree was the most familiar place she could be in, her one shelter. It seemed a slim and tenuous link with her past. It was the place she had come to. Somehow.

Yet she had never believed that the past alone made the future. She had always wanted to venture, to push just a little farther, to go beyond the edge. She had always wanted to go on a spaceship. She would be willing to go and never come back, she had sometimes thought. Though that was not Earth-like. She would go not for adventure or for newness, but for the wonder of it, for the pushing back of walls. Physical walls, quite unlike the idea walls most people worked at.

She had not gone on a spaceship. Her parents were too content on Earth, and she was too young to go alone. The people who did go on spaceships for long distances were mostly older and married, because of the long times of going and coming. So she knew she had not been on a spaceship. She had been in her own world. In a quarry in a green forest, in a place of retreat. A place with an unexpected hole.

The scene around her did not change. The gray-white mistiness was the same. There was no movement. The tree was surely alive. But in all its whiteness, there was no sign of vital flow. Where was she?

She could not stay. If the whole of the place was so misty, so uncertain, so bland and yet so oppressive, she could not stay. She was afraid, and restless. She must move. Picking herself up again carefully, she looked about more searchingly. But with no discernible result. A bump here, a rock there, a small gray-white shrub somewhere else broke the formless pattern, but nothing else, nothing of note. Here was the only tree. The sky too was uniform. More uniform than the ground. There was light, but no difference in light, no deepening colors, no clouds in the uniform depths above. She thought of Earth on a lowering, gray, misty day. Was it this uniform? She thought not. Was this place always thus? Or were there other kinds of days too?

She put one foot in front of the other, moved out from under the tree. The view was the same, in all directions. She had no compass, if a compass would have worked. Nor did she have any other means of direction-finding. She had herself and nothing more. She sighted a bush, as far away as she could see, which was not terribly far, and began to walk. If she could reach that bush, she might see something more appealing to move to. And if not, she could come back to the tree.

The walking was hard. Harder than she had expected. The ground was more solid than she would have imagined. Only under the tree had it been soft. What made walking difficult then? It took several moments to realize that it was the place itself. She was heavy. Too heavy to move easily. She was on a large planet, or a very dense one. Yet she did not think it could be the latter—not when some ground was soft. A large planet then. That was something to know. Larger than Earth. That offered many possibilities. The day, too, might be bigger, longer. But that was harder to be sure of.

The bush was closer, and the horizon had moved beyond it. But there was no change in the landscape. A few more rocks. A few more bumps. And maybe the start of another bush at the edge. She reached her bush and collapsed. She was worn thin. And she had come only a hundred meters or so.

The bush was much like the tree, grayish-white, and the ground beneath it a bit soft. She stayed out on the harder ground.

She was not on her own planet. Unless she was dreaming. Unless the hole had taken her out of her normal consciousness. But would even a fall make such a strange world enter her mind? She felt the ground beside her, pinched herself, wrestled to wake up. And in the end she knew for certain that she was awake, and that somehow, in her flesh, she was elsewhere. It was no time to panic. It was a time for clear thought.

Something inside of her said, "Well, get on with it, girl." Or was it inside? That thought wasn't like her. And what was she to get on with? Pondering? That must be it.

She had been in her lovely world, green and cool and quiet. But not this quiet. Her mind had been busy. There had been that strange thing she had done. The day before. In school. The school head had sent for her, to scold her for gently lifting herself out the window during a class. Everyone could do it, of course. But she had always found it easier than others. Too easy. Just thinking about it sometimes was enough. It happened every once in a while when she was bored. The head had really been angry this time. But the class had been so dull. Pre-Clordian Sweep archaeology didn't interest her very much. She had thought it would, but it didn't. And seeing the outside and wanting it, she had simply gone, because she had willed it. Then while the head had lectured on staying put, she had thought of her hidden corner in the garden near home. She had yearned to be there, physically yearned for it with all her being. It had been a new sort of yearning. She had wanted before, but not like that. And then she had been there. In her flesh, she had been there. It had been too frightening. Lifting up gently and moving out a window was one thing. But being someplace else with no preparation was another. In horror she had yearned with a deep intentness to be back where she had been with the head. And she had been. The head hadn't even missed her. Yet she had been gone. She knew it. For afterward Fraisy had laughed and asked how she'd done it. She'd been outside the window and seen.

She had pondered on that, sitting near the quarry, and then had gone on to think about her cousin Borin. He was something like her, but he was not in school anymore. He was on a spaceship, and she was the only one in the family who really understood why. He needed a physical unknown too. Generally he traveled on a small, short-trip cargo vessel. But lately he had gone on a much longer voyage, with some Core Council people. They had been to a number of planets, making agreements with those who lived there. Back on Earth he had come to tell about it; to tell her mostly, because he knew she cared. And she had listened eagerly. When he left, she had gone to the woods to think about what he had said, about that and about her own strange trip. Yes, that was it. That was what she had done.

She reared up in her thoughts. She was close, close.

"Now you're coming on there." Was it she who had spoken?

No, she was sure it was not. There was someone, something else nearby—but where? It couldn't be just a voice. That was silly. Was it something in another dimension, one she couldn't see? That sounded absurd too. But not so ridiculous as just a voice. Whatever it was, it knew her thoughts and could speak in her language. That in itself was a miracle.

"Not so strange," said the voice. "We sense rather than hear. We transmit ideas, rather than words. You simply make words of ideas to suit your own needs. And we welcome visitors. There is little that is new when you can't move."

"Can't move!" She turned quickly and looked at the bush.

"Of course," it said. "Moving is too hard on this planet. You discovered that yourself. So we are what you call plants, I guess. If by a plant you mean an unmoving living creature with higher sensitivities."

"No, not exactly," she murmured. "Our plants don't talk. Or at least they don't transmit thought."

There was silence for a moment, as if the idea was hard for the bush to understand.

"I grasp, I grasp," came the reply at last. "Then on your world there are moving creatures who think and unmoving creatures who seem not to think. An amazing innovation. A place I'd like to touch. I've heard of things—there are rumors, others of us have encountered things. But I didn't really believe."

"How do you know what others think," she asked, "when none of you can move?"

"Why, we sense each other thinking, of course," the bush replied. "Don't you on your planet sense each other thinking? No, of course you don't. You were surprised at me."

"We speak aloud," she said. "But we don't expect bushes to speak."

"Then maybe that's why they do not speak. No, no, you may be right." The bush sounded apologetic, as if it were at fault in questioning her. Then it was silent. But the silence was filled with thought. It seemed to beg for conversation.

"What planet is this? How do I get home? Where

are you in the galaxy?" They were the first ideas that came to mind. If only she could get some clue, she might find a way to project herself home, she decided. If that was how she had gotten here in the first place.

"Why, how should I know?" asked the bush. "We are where we are. Where I have always been. Why don't you stay? It's nice to have someone so close. I never thought of it before. The winds come and bring pollen from my neighbors, take away the seeds that I have made. I hear the thoughts of my neighbors, and sometimes of the young that I myself have helped create. But we must not grow too close together. We cannot. We need much space beneath the soil. Strange, I think none of us have ever thought how good it might be to have another near. Yet what is, must be. We must grow apart. Still, stay a while, and let us feel together the goodness of the rain that comes quite soon."

She looked across the plain then—to the tree that she had left—the nearest bit of life, and to other bushes, most of them farther than she cared to walk on that heavy world.

"Do you speak often with your neighbors?" she asked.

"There is often something in the air. But not often thoughts as strange as yours. I sense much in you I do not entirely understand. It excites me. It makes me restless. Stay, and ease the strangeness you have brought."

"Bush," she said. "Is it always like this—the gray, the white, the mist, the stillness?"

"Until—until you asked, I would have said what else can there be? But you are here. And in your mind are

136

things that seem strange and frightening. Yet oddly exciting. I have never lacked for thought. I contemplate a stone. There are many that my roots can touch. I think of things I pick from others' thoughts; often there are odd quirks that must be studied. The mists are here, sometimes heavier than now, sometimes lighter when the winds come. There are long thoughts in the mists. Yet not much new as you would sense it. I grasp that now."

"Have you no longings, bush? Do you not wish to know your world at least beyond that tree? Or do you know your world at all?"

"I do not know what your knowing is. I am aware of much, if that is what you mean. The land beyond that tree is like my land here. The stones may differ— new shapes, new sizes. But I do not know all my own stones well, not yet, though my roots reach a long way out. They bring word of new things as they grow a bit now and then—new directions, new earth, new contours, new rock."

The weight of the land was more than the weight of its mass. She saw that now. It was a heavy land, one of stolid immobility. She panicked against it. Yet she did not move. She was too tired with merely the exertion of thought.

She looked down at her lap, then up again at the bush, knowing she must not stay. She must make herself move. The bush might be content, but she needed things she did not find here. It was quiet and alone. She could daydream in peace. Yet she could not stay. She dare not stay. She must eat, for one thing. Though she felt no real hunger as yet.

"I understand. Each of us needs his own kind. Let me enjoy you while I may. Think and I will hear."

"Bush, bush!" she cried. "If only you could see my world. Could know its beauties."

"I cannot. But I have known you."

"Oh, bush, bush, have you seen me? Can you see?"

"In my own fashion. Though not yours, I suspect."

"Then maybe you can grasp my world. If I can get home, I can come again sometime. And maybe I can bring things, let you understand what you can never come to grasp yourself."

"Perhaps." The thought was resigned. The bush did not believe. "Go home. You must, but you will not come again. I will be content. Once, once in my time, a wonder has been near me. That is enough."

She had a feeling the bush was wrong. Having invaded the bush's world, she might have brought discontent forever. She resolved to return even if all the Earth tried to stop her. But first she had to get back to Earth. Her thoughts went back to her cousin Borin and his spaceship. What did that have to do with the place where she was? And how had she come? Was it like floating out of a classroom window? No, it was more like yesterday—the trip to the garden. But how, and why?

Once more she pondered on the green, thick woods of home. The place of noisy quiet. She had started after school, running from Fraisy and Chara. She had gone to think about her own strange adventure and about the places Borin had been. He had seen many solar systems and many planets, minded creatures of many kinds. He had seen other worlds where no one lived.

"There was a white planet," he had said. "With a heavy, breathable atmosphere—a huge planet that held in great clouds of gas and water. We dipped beneath some of those clouds and saw a white surface, bare except for a few almost-white plants. A strange, quiet place. A still, wild world."

She had longed for that planet. It revolved around a star—something in the constellation Crespid. She had thought of her own night sky. She had envisioned the large W in the north and imagined where that star might be in that group. A tree toad had hopped by. Then a chipmunk. And a butterfly had wobbled along. The place she had been was light, too light, too distracting for real thought. There had been a hole nearby, a place of deeper quiet. She had retreated there. And in her mind, in the dark and the stillness, she had conjured up the night sky.

The True Relation of that distant planet in Crespid, that was what she had wanted. Slowly it came back. Yes, a True Relation of 500–20–15–50060321–603212. Borin had written it down. That was it. She could never have remembered it. She had conjured up that world. She had held its True Relation in her mind. What more? Nothing more, except that odd, heightened sense of wanting, of more than wanting, of bending the whole sense of her presence toward something. It was the same as the day before. And then she had pulled herself into oneness in this new world. Was she then at a True Relation of 500–20–15–50060321–603212? On a white planet? And what was the True Relation of Earth? That at least she ought to know. She struggled to remember. And she felt the bush helping her. How, she did not know.

She was sure she would never remember. She decided she would never see Earth again. For it was clear that you had to know—really know—where you were going if you wanted to get there. She had to do more than remember the beauty of Earth, the face of her brother, the look of her home, the marvel of food. She tore her mind apart looking. And the answer eluded her.

"My, you are a busy one, aren't you?" said the bush calmly. "It's a wonder you ever pull yourself together at all."

She quieted then. And in a deep inner peace she let ideas come. Not questing so much as inviting. And eventually the numbers came.

"That's better," said the bush. "Now go home, and don't feel you must keep your promise to return. It may not even be wise."

She did not dispute the voice. She could not. All her thoughts were bent toward reaching that instant of total desire. How did one do it? She worked and nothing happened. Was the planet too heavy to leave? She looked at the bush, at the landscape. Were these to be her life? The bush looked sad, sad in its own way. And she knew in her inner self that it was sad both for her and for itself. It might never again meet the unusual, the unexpected. She looked again at the landscape. Flat and quiet. Too much room for thought here, and maybe too little thought to fill it. Was that her destiny?

They were sad together, the bush and she, until suddenly the wanting in her grew greater than she had ever known. It was a wanting of two together, a wanting mixed with parting and sadness. Could such wanting go on forever?

It was dark around her then. Did it grow dark so quickly on that strange planet? For the first time she reached to touch the bush and felt instead a wall, a dirt wall. Was she where she had been—on Earth—the hole she had left? She had given the True Relation; she had held the latitude and longitude of her place as close as she knew it; she had conjured up the roads and the paths from town. Was that enough?

On all fours, she crawled ahead in the dark until at last she saw a light, very dim. She moved out into that light, the last of daylight. It was not the same woods. But yes it was! The woods were a great belt along the low hills that ringed the town. This was another part of them. She knew it. It was a part she loved, but one that was too far from home for an afternoon's jaunt. Even the hole she remembered now. Another remnant of the days of mining. She even knew where the road was, the old road, almost overgrown, that people took to come here now and then. Kids from old-fashioned families that still insisted on sequestering often came out here.

She stood up, took a step, and moved more quickly than she had planned. She fell and skinned her knee. It hurt, and she wondered if she could walk as far as she must to get home. Yet she couldn't stay in the woods all night. It would get cold, and she didn't have even a coat. Besides, the woods were too alone, too quiet and yet not quiet enough, especially after the place she had been. She needed to go home.

She stood up once more and, holding herself steady and slow, moved toward the road. She felt jumpy and tired and not quite herself. In a panic she tried to run, and fell again, hurting the same knee and the other as well. Misery lurked all around, and she sought frantically for a way out of it.

"My, you are a busy one." The words were as clear in her mind as when the bush had thought them at her. Yet it had to be memory. Once more she grew quiet.

And then the solution was obvious. If she could think herself to a planet in the constellation Crespid, she could think herself home. Of course she could. But once having thought of it, she found she was almost too tired to do it. She panicked again. Then let herself grow calm. Pulled all of herself in. And then she was ready. She thought of home, of the relation of home to the place where she was, the roads and the distances. And she wanted it. Oh, how she wanted it. And all at once, it worked. She was outside her own door.

She was late for dinner, of course.

"Menta, where in the world have you been?" her mother cried, more in relief than in anger. Generally she would have replied with silence, or said some noncommittal thing. She liked her privacy. And her mother knew it. The whole family knew it too well. But now she could not just let it pass.

"To the woods," she said. "I fell," she added, "and had trouble getting home."

"Menta," her mother said, half in fear for her and half in a real attempt to understand, "you simply cannot go off like that. Something really bad could happen to you. Those woods are full of old holes. You know that. And you know you never look where you're going. You could fall into something and never get out. And we wouldn't know where to find you. Why do you do it?"

"You needn't worry about me, not now," Menta said, looking at her mother, understanding her as never before and loving her with a kind of giving love that was new and exciting.

"Whatever do you mean by that?" her mother asked in a sharper tone. Then she looked at Menta, really looked, and an odd expression came over her face. "Menta, has something happened to you? Something, something. . . ." She did not finish, but she seemed disturbed. "Hurry and clean up. I'll have your dinner ready when you come down."

Menta grinned. "I'm starved," she said.

Later, after she ate, she tried to explain, just to her mother, what had happened. She was too tired to even think of demonstrating. And her mother was too amazed to think it was anything but a fairy tale, a dream, a result of falling, maybe.

And so it remained. Menta did not speak of it again. Her mother watched her closely, she knew. And she knew that her mother was perplexed. For she had been right, there was a change. And even she didn't know why or what. She was more whole, more herself. She was quiet, and yet she no longer needed a place apart, a wild freedom in the woods and hills. She had it inside herself, where she had strange memories to ponder.

She reached out to others more. Like her friend the bush, she tried to know and understand the stones around her. And with her roots and her mind, she sought the meanings that lay in her own tight world. They produced riches she had never dreamed existed.

Her father, her mother, her brother were people with a dimension she had never anticipated. Even school became different. She saw it as the bush would have seen it, savored it as that bush would have done.

She used the power sparingly, but she did use it. She did not want to forget how. Yet she took only small jumps to places she knew. She yearned to visit the bush again. But something inside her was afraid. What would happen if she went to the wrong place? Sometimes in her mind-moving, as she came to think of it, she did wind up in a place she had not chosen. Why, she could not be sure. What would happen if she found herself on a dangerous planet, or even a star? Yet she yearned to speak once more to a bush, to share that sort of wisdom.

Eventually her cousin Borin came to visit again. He had been on a short shuttle trip to Clord. He came with more restlessness in him than ever before. As if that one long trip into far space had left him unable to be content with less.

The first night he was there, after the evening meal, Menta had to speak. "Borin, I've thought a lot about that strange planet you saw, the white one. Can you show me where in Crespid it is?"

Her mother looked at her strangely, as if she thought the odd dream-adventure had long been forgotten. It had never been mentioned after that first night, though it had been clear that she herself had not forgotten it. The strange careful looks she had given Menta had been enough to display that. Now there was nothing she could say. She had to let them go to see the constellation. Menta was glad that no questions could be asked.

Menta and Borin walked down to an open field at the edge of the town and sat looking toward the north. There, looking toward her planet, for she had begun to feel that way about it, she told Borin the tale of her adventure. And he didn't believe her.

"Menta," he said, "you fell. You were dazed, and you dreamed."

"But I came back in another place," she said. "And I've done short trips around here since."

"No, you're having some sort of delusions."

She was desperate. Someone had to believe her, and he had been her one hope. She had waited for him, believing that he would understand. Hardly knowing what she did, she concentrated on the school yard and instantly found herself there; it was deserted and quiet as it never was in the day. She waited a minute or two, then brought herself back to Borin. When she returned, he was standing, looking around. But her agony was only increased because he was sure she had tricked him.

"Menta, you've learned some clever tricks, and somehow you've gotten a good impression of a planet that fascinated me, but you can't convince me of anything more." He laughed.

Once more she disappeared. This time, although she hated to do it, she put herself at home in the room where the family was gathered. Her father saw her and her mother and her brother. They were wondering aloud what had happened to the two of them, and there she was. But only long enough for her to nod at them and return to the edge of town. Her powers of concentration had improved for her to be able to do that, she realized. What a shame no one believed her.

Again Borin laughed when she was back beside him. "You must teach me that trick sometime," he said.

"I'd like to," she cried. And then she changed the subject. They walked home talking of things in a casual way, and he, at least, was unprepared for the stir the two of them created when they walked into the house.

"Menta," said her father, "if you go for a walk with Borin to see the stars, you ought at least to stay with him. There was no call for you to come home alone. And why didn't you answer when I spoke to you? Where did you go so quickly?"

Her mother was silent. Borin looked at her in awe. But even so his mind was quick. "She ran in to get me a range finder," he said. "I'd forgotten it."

Her parents turned away then, as if the explanation had been given. But she could sense that they were puzzled. Borin said nothing more. She went off to do some schoolwork, and he to his ever-present calculations. You'd think, she had often said, that he'd never heard of a computer. But he always replied that it took a sharp mind to keep a computer alert on a short journey. And besides, he liked calculations. They kept him awake. The men watched two weeks on and two weeks off on short trips. And it could be dull, Menta supposed. She decided she liked her way of travel better, even if it might not always be so dependable. She wondered how soon it would be before he appeared to ask questions.

Eventually he came to the door of her room and opened it a crack, whispering through as if he didn't want others to hear what he said. "Menta, I've got to talk to you. You know that, don't you? And you know I'm sorry."

She nodded. "Tomorrow," she said.

The next day Borin met her after school. They walked off to the woods, the place she'd first gone to, and she told him, all over again, the whole story. This time in more detail because he wanted to know every bit of it.

"Tell me again how your mind sets," he said at the end.

She explained it once more, and then again.

"It's as if you were breaking into another compartment of your mind," she said finally. "Or maybe breaking into a new kind of being." The last she whispered. She had hardly said it before, even to herself. Yet she had been different, ever since that day.

He tried and tried and nothing happened.

"Do it for me again," he said.

She quieted, drew into herself. Then she thought of home, and there she was. She still had her school films in her hand, so she dropped them on the table inside the door. Then she took herself back to Borin. It was hard to place herself exactly in the midst of a forest, so she arrived about forty meters from him. He watched her walk toward him.

"What is the secret?" he asked, puzzled.

"It's the quiet, I think," she said. "And the wanting, the really wanting. It's wanting to be there that matters. Not wanting to do it."

He looked even more puzzled. Then he relaxed and sat back. He motioned for her to sit beside him, and she did. They talked of many things. Until all at once he was still. And then he wasn't there. He didn't return for at least ten minutes, and she began to be afraid that he had gone way off and couldn't get back. But finally he was beside her, chuckling.

"Got caught with your mother," he said. "She's worried about you. You're in and out so fast these days. And you seem different."

Menta laughed with him. It was a warm, rich, understanding laugh. For they now shared a dimension known, as far as they could tell, to no one but themselves. They were unique. It was frightening, but it also gave them a warm sense of comradeship. She left secure, knowing that Borin would learn more, would perhaps tell a few others. And there would be trips with others someday. Safer trips than she could make alone. Maybe even a trip to a certain white planet, to see a very important bush.

THE TALKAROUND

Not many people these days remember Jalish Dozent. Except that he did something strange when he was young—and that he wandered around a whole lot in the galaxy. Not many remember what he found, and their forgetting is not entirely an accident.

It's true that Jalish Dozent was young, purely and simply young, when he took off that first time for someplace else. Most that go, even now, are twenty, maybe twenty-five, before they make even little jumps away. And then they don't stay for long. They don't make a vacation of it; it's just a short adventure or a brief research expedition. It isn't that they can't go younger, of course—that they don't have the roots of it. It's just that no one lets them do it. There are all those controls still. Just as there were in Jalish's time.

Then too, the inner searchings, the unity of Earth life, have always made travel by the young seem unwise. And other planets have always had their own reasons for keeping the young at home. For example, there's always been the thought that the young might not be able to cope if they came into a really rough spot. It's a handy idea, so although it's never been proved, it stays around. There are other reasons, some sensible and some not, why the young cannot leave their own planets. And so, things being as they are and were, it wasn't really so amazing that Jalish managed to go where he went as it was surprising that he got to do it at all. He was sixteen at the time.

By the year it happened, all the space-oriented planets, even the ones where the minded species hadn't yet gotten the knack of self-space-placement, had the usual psychic screens around them so one couldn't just project from planet to planet whenever one wanted. They were cruder screens then than the ones now in use, more like the ones people have to shelter their homes; still, they were effective. People could come and go, but they had to get a permit, and they had to schedule the opening of any screen they wanted to go through. Much like now.

Screens have always created some nuisances, but people have always thought the safety was worth the trouble. In fact, as far as some of the people then were concerned, the screens saved a lot of difficulty. There were still those who remembered the days before screens had become universal, and they could still conjure up the horrors of it. People had gone jumping around and no one had ever been sure of who or what might turn up within a hundred meters or so. It was almost impossible to try to find somebody, because everybody was always off someplace else. It was a craze even Earth people fell for. The screens and the permits and the records cleaned all that up.

So even if the screens did put a damper on people's free travel, in the end only a few Universal Movement Association members stayed upset about the new situ-

ation. And kids complained too. They had the hardest
time getting permits. Like now, they were taught from
the time they started school, at three, how to get
around. By the time they were nine or ten, they were
as good as adults—they could pinpoint themselves almost anywhere they wanted on the home planet. By
sixteen the galaxy, or the near parts, the local sectors,
could have been open. But they weren't. And lots of
kids didn't like it. Even Earth kids, who realized more
than most that the far and the near can have a unity
that nullifies distance.

Some people thought after Jalish made his trip that
the Universal Movement Control Agency had simply
tried to make an example of him to keep the kids
quiet. But anyone who knew Jalish didn't really think
that. They knew he'd just done his usual job of getting
what he wanted when he wanted it. Jalish could talk
himself into or out of almost anything.

It really started the day Jalish was late to cosmology class. Not that that mattered. Teachers seldom
cared if Jalish was late. It gave them a few minutes
alone with the class. Anyway, that day the class was
up at one of Earth's astronomy satellites, checking out
some far parts of the galaxy. It was a double period
class—10 to 12 Earth time. Jalish had stopped off before
taking himself up to the satellite to ask the movement
teacher (that's where he'd been the class before—
in movement) a whole spill of questions. The kind
that made teachers hate to see him come, though
most did take him with good grace. He was a nice
enough kid, after all. And he really meant those questions. He actually wanted to know. The trouble was
that most of the time no one had the answers. This

teacher hemmed and hawed around until Jalish was late to cosmology class.

As it turned out, he hadn't missed a thing. He'd gotten acquainted with the parts of the galaxy they were looking at that day when he was eight. But he listened to the teacher, once he'd settled in, with half a mind anyway, just in case he might have a question. The rest of his mind was taking in everything he could see through the huge ceiling lens. It was maybe an hour down the line, halfway through the class time, when it happened.

The lens was sweeping from one part of the Milky Way to another, and as it went, Jalish got a fleeting impression of a pink and green star. When he thought about it later, he wasn't even sure he had seen it. Just felt it was there. It seemed a bit odd, to say the least, and it didn't take Jalish long to figure out just where it had to be, if it actually existed, the True Relation. He was a genius at True Relations, even at sixteen. The star was outside the core of the galaxy, where even he had sense enough not to want to go, but not far out. Maybe because it was so close to the core, it was in an area that was almost always marked "mostly unexplored" on galactic survey maps. There were a lot of places like that in those days, of course, but this was an unusually large one.

No one had been able to explain to Jalish why this huge unexplored patch existed, or why any existed at all. It had always surprised him that anything outside the core had not been visited by someone. The young don't always grasp the size of things or the complexities of going to out-of-the-way places. But Jalish, more than most, wondered why when people went someplace they went to a place they knew. That just didn't make sense to him. When he left Earth, it would be for some decent purpose, like investigating an unexplored solar system.

Anyway, by the time Jalish left that class, he had his mind made up. He was going to find out if that pink and green star existed, and he also intended to go there, if what he discovered made it appear to be even one-tenth as strange as it seemed to him then. The more he thought about it, the more peculiar the whole thing got. Though the star had looked odd enough, that wasn't the end. It had seemed almost to make a sound. Nonsense, of course, but he couldn't shake the idea, and it raised all kinds of questions in his mind that, as usual, had no answers.

Sitting in the eating room back on Earth, he pondered; after eating he went to the library. There he checked tapes and holographic photographs made by research expeditions. A star was there, where he had placed the True Relation. No question of that. The sky maps showed it, though he could find nothing much written about it. And—this became the major issue for him then—it was not shown as being pink and green. It was a plain yellow sun. Yet he knew it was pink and green. He was convinced of it.

There was a time discrepancy between the research material and his own look at the star. Did that matter? Of course it did. The research material was newer, taken closer. It made a difference. The star might once have been pink and green and now be yellow. But even that didn't make sense. It didn't fit any pattern of star development he had ever heard of.

Before he crawled into bed that night, he had

checked again to make sure of his True Relation. Everything was in order. He'd been looking up the right star. And he'd found everything known about it. It was such a deep void star, it didn't even have a number, much less a name. And no one was sure it had a planet, although it was the right magnitude for planets, and its motion seemed to indicate that some were likely. For no reason he could determine, Jalish was sure it did have them. Yet all that he had discovered had only added to the questions that he needed to have answered; and it was obvious that no one was going to be able to help him. For once he was not going to be satisfied with evasions. He was going to go to one of the planets of the pink and green star. Having made his decision, Jalish went to sleep.

There was no one at school the next day who could give him permission to go. He had known that even before he asked. But he had to begin there. His space action teacher said maybe he ought to go to the Remote Regions Guidance Council. As far as the teacher was concerned, it was a place to send him, a way of achieving a morning's rest. Jalish went at once. He was at the council office immediately. And there they finally sent him on to Remote Space Missions, where they said he didn't qualify for their programs and he ought to go to Youth in Space. It was the man there who pushed him off onto the Universal Movement Control Agency. The feeling was that the UMCA permitters were tough enough to send him home. No one else had quite managed that.

But the UMCA had had too many young ones coming in with arguments for going off to someplace else. It seemed as if the under-twenty crowd was the only group that hadn't settled into the typical Earth pattern of deep focus on inner matters, and of staying at home except when there was good reason for leaving. Life would have been dull at the agency if it hadn't been for the kids, but they were the ones who couldn't go anywhere. It seemed a shame sometimes, the permitters thought. Most of the still-in-schools would have been scared to go much beyond Uranus or Pluto—a harmless jaunt. But even that couldn't be done, so the whole thing was a perpetual nuisance.

Jalish, though he was something of a novelty, proved more a trial than a nuisance. To begin with, he was more persistent than most. And he was persuasive. The extent of his knowledge was alarming, and he used it like no one at the agency had heard before. His mother wore ear plugs or turned up the white noise full blast when Jalish really wanted something. But the UMCA people didn't know about that. And finally, they didn't know how—short of easing him out of his mind for a while, which wasn't allowed either—they were ever going to get rid of him.

At last they called his school for advice. That was, after all, where he belonged. It was also a mistake. The school recommended the trip. It had been such a pleasant day there with Jalish gone. Everyone had relaxed.

Next the UMCA called his mother. She sometimes worked at home, and that's where she was that day. But she'd forgotten to turn down the white noise, and she didn't really hear the request. She understood that it was something about Jalish. A permission for something. And since, as far as she knew, he was at school and the school must know what it was doing, she said yes.

There was no further recourse. The UMCA permitters put the usual space gear on Jalish, the equipment they had on hand for trips to blank spots—oxygen and a cosmic ray shield and all the rest. Enough to get him through a couple of minutes at a planet near his pink and green star and back again, even if it was as dangerous as they thought it might be. Then they let him go, with the usual warning to come back soon and not to be swallowed by monsters.

One minute he was there with them laughing. And the next minute he was on the fifth planet of the pink and green star. Why the fifth planet? Well, he didn't know for sure just how many planets there were. Why should he? No one else even knew if there were planets at all. It had just seemed a good place to aim for, and he had worked out a reasonable True Relation. He had no real basis for what he did, and yet he had felt sure of himself. Why, he did not know. Even Jalish sometimes knew when questions were useless.

The UMCA people were sure Jalish would be back in five minutes or so, disappointed and quiet. But they were wrong. After an hour they began to worry. He had seemed so intelligent, and so persistent, they had never dreamed he would get lost—forget the way home. They began to wonder if they should send someone after him. But when they stopped to think, they realized they didn't know where he had gone. A pink and green planet. Whoever heard of such a thing? And where in the galaxy? What was the True Relation? They called up the school in a real panic when two hours had passed, but no one there could help them, not even the cosmology teacher. Who could pick out a single star in the sweep of a lens? Only Jalish.

They called his mother, but she still had the white noise on and was no help at all. His father didn't even know Jalish had wanted to go anywhere, let alone that he had already gone. He yelped when he heard, and the next minute he was right there at UMCA. He didn't blame anyone. He knew Jalish too well. He just wanted to add his brain to the tangle. A whole crew began to work on the problem.

At that moment, for a change, Jalish wasn't thinking nearly so hard as they were. In fact, there wasn't a question in his mind. He'd outdone himself at last. He'd found a place that left him speechless and empty.

When he had first come, there had been the colors. Not just pink and green, but all colors. The star seemed to emit light of every color in the spectrum, though Jalish knew that wasn't how things worked. But he didn't start trying to figure it out. He just looked. At the star, and at the fifth planet where his feet were. The whole planet was jumping with color. Not just in the sky. There were tall waves of color sweeping back and forth over the ground. Some were big—sixty, eighty meters high—he estimated. Others were smaller. And the space between was white. A white you felt without its being anything you would touch. What vegetation there was, was sparse and a shiny gray. These gray things caught the color and reflected it. Electromagnetic waves of some sort—a giant aurora—was the thought that flashed into his mind a few moments after he landed. And then he stopped thinking.

He simply had no thoughts of his own. The waves filled his mind, and not only color waves, but music waves as well. Because there was music too. It all came into his mind, and there was no room left for anything else. The music moved with the waves of light, keeping time with them. Each wave had a beat of its own, and yet all the waves worked together. And together they really rocked him. They took over and left him standing there with nothing at all going on inside. And that's how it still was two hours after he came.

Eventually he sat down and leaned back against one of the big flat-bladed gray plants, a little like a cactus he'd seen once. But he hardly knew what he was doing. He was only a little part of a big color and a big sound. He didn't know anything else existed, not even himself.

Later, a lot later, his mind began to creep back underneath and around the sides of the waves that were still in the middle. It took a little pressure, a little force to do it, but there was something in Jalish that never could leave well enough alone; he had to push against things. So he made a wedge for himself, and his thoughts began to take shape; it occurred to him then that all that sound wasn't just sound. It was music, but it wasn't just music. The light was color, but not just color.

He pushed a bit farther and it hit him that all that sight and sound might be what passed for people on that planet. It was about the second real thought he'd had on the fifth planet, and at first he was afraid he'd lost his mind entirely. Usually a new thought like that picked Jalish up and left him feeling pretty good, but this one just left him sitting, lower and lower, if possible. The problem was that if he was right, he had no way of knowing what was going to happen to him. When the waves sort of bounced up and down a little harder and the sound took on a pleasant murmur, he could feel he was right. But that still didn't give him a clue to his future, if he had one, or to when he might have his whole mind back again.

That was only the beginning. It took a while longer before Jalish really got a sense of what was going on. And when he did, he felt almost worse than before. He knew then that he had put himself in a real mess. Because it was clear that those waves were pumping his mind. All his questions and all his answers were being siphoned out. Everything he'd ever known. Or rather, it was all being absorbed. The waves had come in and were just soaking it up. There was no real need for language. The waves didn't use it. His mind waves simply blended with their mind waves. Were these people, if you could call them that, all mind? Were the waves themselves mind? He couldn't think that far. There wasn't room enough for his thoughts to work that out. So he just sat and let it all happen. It wasn't usual with Jalish to let things go like that, but this wasn't a usual situation.

And soon things became even more unusual. Because Jalish almost relaxed. And with that, he actually felt the waves prodding around in his mind. And because he sensed them there, for the first time he really understood something of what they were. That was when he nearly blew apart. Energy, nothing but energy. Not even atoms, really. Waves of particles. Something so basic that the whole universe seemed contained in just one. What they knew seemed to go all the way back to the big bang his cosmology teacher liked to explain, maybe even to something before. Though that was hard to think about. He sensed it all, breathed it in through his mind, absorbed it, and then he nearly collapsed. For the first time in his life he was not in charge.

Once they all knew each other better, that is, once the waves had taken in everything Jalish had on his mind, including the fact that he dimly perceived what they were, more of the waves came closer. They crowded around him and all but ran up against him. He felt them, and yet he didn't. Of course he had the suit on; but there was a gentle pressure here and there on the outside. They were really giving him the once over, he decided. And sometimes he dimly sensed that they didn't wholly believe what they had found, anymore than he believed what he had found. It was hard for them to admit that he was as solid as he was, though of course they could move right through him; and it was even harder for them to accept his thoughts, especially the idea that there were lots more like him, back where he came from. This seemed to scare them. The lights and the music began to clash and to move a bit faster. But eventually the uproar settled, and it seemed as if they had decided to live with what they had learned, after all.

After a while the waves made it clear that they wanted Jalish to stand up and go along on a little trip. They flicked all around him, and he could see that he didn't have much choice. They might be transparent, but he had an idea they had a lot of power within them; this was an idea he thought it was better not to check out.

The planet had a glossy, solid surface, which the waves slid over rather smoothly as they squired him along. There was water, or something of the sort, here and there, and the strange gray plants were scattered around. Once in a while they passed a huge chunk of raw metal, big as a house, barren and a bit rusty looking. And other times there were odd-looking stones. Jalish tried to store away pictures of everything he saw.

It began to get dark as they moved, and Jalish was unreasonably glad that the planet was like other planets at least in that way. But even in the dark the waves went on, a little darker maybe, but still there. They now cast strange shadows on the ground.

Moving forward, Jalish felt more and more of his mind coming back. The waves were through searching it at last, he guessed. But he was still too stunned, and too tired now, to think very much. He did decide he wasn't really afraid any longer, and he wasn't in much danger. In fact, it was all rather nice by that time—the music and the lights. He was used to it, and he liked it. The only thing he needed was a bit of supper.

That was what actually made him decide it was time to go home. With his mind back, he could think of things like that if he wanted to. So with a real jerk on himself, he pulled in and set things up for going. He hated to, in a way. But he couldn't just stay. He tried to think out an explanation to the waves around him, a sort of apology for running off, and then he put himself in mind to leave. But nothing happened. The usual system didn't work. He didn't move a meter toward home. And that's when he really discovered what it means to be afraid. He could see that he'd soon know what hunger really was, too. And more than that, he decided he was homesick. It was all very fine to go away, but home had its advantages if you hadn't planned for a long stay, which he hadn't.

The waves, he saw, understood what was happening. They crowded around, as if to keep him cool and happy. Still he might have given way to a real case of the shakes if the biggest wave he had seen all day hadn't suddenly come bolting in. It hit down right there in front of him, gently. And then he understood. They'd sent for the head wave—if that's what this was.

It was the same round all over. His mind was borrowed again, and he could only guess what questions and what answers they were waving out of it. All perfectly friendly, but at the same time more than a little wearing, especially when you were hungry. That was a thing the waves didn't seem to understand. It slipped into him finally that if they ate anything at all it would be natural field forces or cosmic rays or something of that type. Not especially appetizing. Probably didn't even come in different flavors. He almost laughed. Even pills would be better.

The search was over all at once. The head wave backed off and left. The waves all drew back in a circle, the ones that were left. They bowed, that was all he could call it, and waited around him, as if something was about to happen. And at that instant Jalish realized that for the first time since he had landed, he truly had all of his mind back, including the part that

could take him home. He was so pleased, he bowed in
return. And at the same moment questions flooded in,
not their questions, but his. It was his turn now, he
decided. No sense in going back so soon, even if he
was hungry. He hadn't come all that way and gone
through all that for nothing. But when he began to try
to ask the things he felt he had to know, the waves
were gone. In despair he realized that there was nothing he could do now but go home. He'd never felt so
frustrated, so utterly defeated, in his life. Obviously
these waves had never heard of fair play. They had
called him. That was the only way he had seen the
star as pink and green from Earth. Though how they
had done it, he couldn't say. And now, without doing
anything for him, they had left him. He set himself up
for home, and the next thing he knew he was in the
UMCA office.

It looked the same, yet not the same. What was
wrong?

To begin with. everyone there was just a little too
solid. Once he got over that shock, Jalish decided that
no one looked as if he or she had eaten for at least
twelve hours or slept for twenty-four. Which was more
or less the truth of it. Some word of Jalish's trip had
leaked out, and what worry hadn't done, questions
from the outside had. The Core Council was in
steady contact, and the local Sector Group had been
warned in case Jalish got stuck in someone else's
screen. With all that, everyone there looked half dead,
and was. Each agency officer in the room was so
wrapped up in one little corner of the problem that no
one saw Jalish for at least three minutes. And then no
one had strength enough to say anything. For Jalish it

was like being back on the fifth planet again, only harder. This time he had to talk.

When things finally settled down, and everyone had had a late supper, Jalish showed them where he'd been. The showing wasn't hard. It was the telling that took time. There wasn't an easy thing to believe in the whole strange story. But Jalish stuck to the truth, and since no one could prove it wasn't the truth, UMCA and everyone else finally had to believe.

Of course, when word really got out, the experts came tumbling in, and then Jalish had his hands full. What helped him most at that point were all the things he knew. There were things in his mind that had never been in anyone's mind before, at least not in any mind on Earth or in the immediate sector. The more he probed around, the more he found. He had so many ideas and so many questions that were so new that nobody could doubt he'd been some place strange. Slowly it dawned on him that while those waves had been in there probing, he'd picked up a whole lot from them in return. It hadn't been a one-sided venture after all. He had learned things about the whole system that nobody on any planet anyone had visited had ever learned before. The experts looked at him in awe.

They made him a Universal Spokesman and a Man of Honor in cosmology, planetology, radiology, and various branches of primary matter study and energy concerns, all at the same time. Then to both Jalish's and the school's relief, it was decided that he didn't have to finish even quarter school. He knew more than almost anyone—about some things, anyway—and he was still only sixteen.

When they finally left him alone, there was no doubt about his being able to do anything he wanted to do. His whole life was ahead of him, and he was on his own to shape it.

What he did was to start watching the pink and green star—the planet, of course, couldn't be seen from any-place reasonable for observation. Others went with him to the nearest possible observation post, and everyone agreed that the star was pink and green. But it seemed dimmer to him than it had before. And as time went by, this proved to be the case. The pink and green dimmed until it was finally gone, and a plain old yellow star was left. Other scientists were puzzled, but not Jalish. He'd seen those waves whipping back and forth up there. And he'd sensed how upset they'd been over what they'd learned from him. So he knew they'd decided they didn't want to be visited again, not for a while, anyway. It was why he hadn't gone back. He had sensed that they were afraid of solid creatures. All that was clear. The only real question was: Were the planets and the star empty? Yes, he decided, the waves had gone. They had simply picked up and moved. But where?

The whole problem made Jalish uneasy. He really wanted to think that his friends (he'd come to think of them as friends; after all, they'd gotten him out of school and into something much better) were all still someplace. But he didn't know how to find them. For the second or third time in his life, he was really baffled. He felt he had to find some waves again. Others, perhaps, that weren't afraid. He had to know more about them. They alone had the answers to the questions that still filled his mind. Questions about the galaxy and about the universe, but most of all questions about the waves themselves. How old were they? Were they all different, or were they all basically alike? Did they have more than one sex? Were there children? And if he found some again, would they answer his questions? Would they let him come near them? Obviously the ones he had met already knew all he knew, and they hadn't liked some of what they saw. Would they or any others be willing to take him in again?

As time passed, his attention gradually moved to other unexplored places in the galaxy. He mapped huge uncharted regions, exploring tirelessly, always by himself. He was free to go whenever he chose, and he was always snapping out to really wild places, and coming home with strange stories, all of which made him pretty much an outer galactic hero. But he was never really satisfied. Those who knew him best said he'd never have a quiet day until he found another pink and green solar system. Not that another would be the same, maybe. But he wanted another chance at some of those waves, whatever the color. He didn't know for sure what would happen if he found some. But he was willing to take a chance.

They still don't let sixteen-year-olds off their home planets much. And it still makes some of them mad. But then there aren't too many people anymore who remember Jalish Dozent's first trip. Everyone in the fifty sectors of the galactic arms lives by some of his ideas and discoveries. But few remember that so much came out of one trip made by one sixteen-year-old. To the few who do remember, it seems wiser that the others do not.

A CENTRAL QUESTION

Ganser Wekot looked up at the sky—close, encircling, and too enticing. It was too much like home. Strange that the sky on Cora C should remind him so of Earth. Though maybe not. Cora C was about the same distance from its sun as Earth was from its. And the suns were near in size. The atmospheres were remarkably similar; physically he'd adapted easily. So it was understandable, the similarity in the sky. Still, he hated it, hated to be reminded of Earth.

Most of those who'd come to the Outer Galactic Council's new school for service trainees were content. They didn't seem to have the affection for their home planets that he did. Yet there was Bilee from Groad and Flu-on from Xenos D. They weren't really happy on Cora C either. He'd mentioned the sky to them; but they saw other things. For Bilee it was the rocks: same colors, same cut as Groad. For Flu-on it was the wind: always sharp the way it was on Xenos D. The three of them had tried to like the school, tried to like the place where they found themselves, to adjust as the others had, but somehow they simply could not.

They had been on Cora C for two years, but it seemed a lot longer. Ganser hadn't wanted to come;

he had had no choice. His mother was Council Leader for Sector 5, and so he had had to set an example when he was chosen. He had wondered why, and still did. It was his mother's job to lead, not his.

Each one of the fifty sectors of the outer galaxy had been asked to send two or three of their young—only two or three, so it was very selective—to the school. It was experimental, as was almost everything the council undertook. After all, the council itself was new. It was just exploring means to unify the outer galactic sectors into doing some things together. The students at the school, when they finished their training, would carry out special galaxy-wide projects. They were being taught to look at the outer galaxy as a whole, something few representatives from any minded species were equipped to do. Ganser wasn't sure that he and his schoolmates were going to be much better equipped, but he guessed someone had to at least try.

On Earth everyone beyond a certain level in school had had to take the exams the council had sent around, for choosing those who would come to the school. He had had the feeling that they especially wanted someone from Earth, though why he wasn't sure. At any rate, he had been chosen. Why that had happened, he wasn't sure either. Maybe since he knew so much about sector government, because of his mother. Most people on Earth didn't pay too much attention to governments of any kind. And now Earth was half a galaxy away. And it was likely to remain that way even during their short school vacations, with travel controls so tight.

Lately the whole outer galaxy had gotten so precise about travel; it didn't make sense. He knew there were dangers. You could accidentally land in the wrong place and be in trouble. And some minds got upset on long trips—bodies even. So there had to be protection, he supposed. But not to let anyone go anywhere at all. That didn't seem reasonable.

"Ganser, you haven't made a sound in ten minutes."

Ganser grinned at Bilee. "It's the sky today. It's—well, it makes me think too much. I'm not really here."

Bilee grinned back. She looked around at the broad flat gravel plain, the steep brown cliffs in the distance, and the deep blue vegetation that made small circles here and there. "Fillets on your sky. Give me good brown stone anytime."

They both laughed out loud.

"What's the meeting for tonight?" Ganser asked, changing the subject. It wasn't often the whole school was called together. But word had been passed down at the midday meal that there was to be a big meeting tonight. And nothing had been the same the rest of the day. Flu-on hadn't even been able to come walking. He was stuck setting up the amphitheater.

Bilee shrugged. "Some visiting wonder, I suppose," she said. "Some Outer Galactic Council member. Or maybe a Sector Council Leader."

Ganser toyed with the idea. His mother, maybe? The idea flooded him with anticipation. He hadn't seen anyone in his family in two years. But then he shrugged it off. The meeting might not be because of visitors at all. And even if it were, the chance of his mother being there was remote.

"Your mother hasn't said she was coming, has she?" Bilee asked, all but reading his thoughts.

"She wouldn't tell me if she were coming," he said. "It wouldn't be right, with others not knowing."

Ganser's thoughts bounded away again. Why did Earth people need each other so much, when others didn't seem to have the same need? Why did Earth people seem so drawn toward home? It wasn't that they didn't like to travel. Most went off on business or pleasure now and then and enjoyed it. And a few found space absolutely fascinating. Yet Earth always called them back.

His mind turned to some of the jaunts he had made with his Uncle Britter before he had come to Cora C, before travel restrictions had become so tight. He'd spent a lot of time with his Aunt Kirry and Uncle Britter, because both of his parents were gone a good deal. He and Uncle Britter had often traveled to strange places for a day or two. It had been fun, even if his mother hadn't always approved when she found out. Uncle Britter could make any trip an adventure, but some of the ones they had shared together had given him experiences he would never forget. Uncle Britter liked odd planets. Yet, no matter how exciting a trip had been, the coming home had always been a joy. There was warmth, a welcoming feeling about Earth that no other planet shared.

"I hope it's not a lecture," Bilee said suddenly. "I'm so tired of sitting. It's too settled here. All those classes on problems of the galaxy where we just talk. Yet it's not peaceful here either, really. All those minds are always pushing at you, for no reason."

Ganser looked over sympathetically. He hadn't really known that she felt it so strongly, the weariness of sitting and learning and never doing. Coming from

Groad, she was square and firm, built for action. And of course her four arms made it obvious that her race did things.

"I don't mind learning," Ganser said slowly. "I like to know things. It's being stuffed with it until you could explode and never being given a chance to make something happen. Some of the others here seem like blotters; they soak up everything that's given them and never stop, but it all stays just where it's put. They never get beyond their endless dead-end games. We're not like that home, and it's hard for me to understand."

Bilee shrugged. "Better start back. If we're too late, they'll keep us in tomorrow."

That was true, although the school had shown the three of them unusual consideration when their restlessness had become apparent. Sometimes some of the teachers had almost seemed to approve.

They turned and ran toward the low flat building—mostly roofs, since the largest part of the school was underground—in the distance. Unable to talk, not wanting to think, Ganser ran toward the sky—the sky over the buildings.

Flu-on met them at the door, at the bottom of the steps.

"Where have you been? You're almost late for dinner."

Ganser shrugged. Food here didn't interest him. Mostly concentrates with a few tasteless bulk items to make those who needed them feel full.

The three moved to the room that served as a mess hall and generally as an assembly room as well, though tonight they were to meet in the more formal amphitheater. The meal was eaten quickly and almost in silence, though there was an electric quality to the air. Only twice before had there been a formal general assembly, and neither of them had been called suddenly.

Ganser looked around, studying the others. Most of them were busy all the time with their minds, looking for ways to test themselves against other minds or soaking up information that would help them when they did find an opponent. They did not need to move much physically, yet each seemed to be struggling for space, mental space. They seemed to define themselves by pushing against others, yet it didn't seem to matter who the others were. Earth people, on the other hand, found themselves inside, and worked with others who shared their interests to discover new things. Was that why he felt himself so different here?

Yet tonight the rest did not seem so different. He sensed around him a reflection of his own curiosity and more than a vague apprehension about the meeting to be held. He didn't know why he felt as he did. Did they? What were they afraid of? Maybe they knew something he didn't. They soaked up knowledge, and in spite of their combativeness, they did sometimes use their knowledge in interesting ways, creating patterns and puzzles and hypothetical situations that were really fascinating. And they were not all alike, even though sometimes they did seem almost like building blocks, each occupying a given space and filling a given function. Maybe underneath they were more like him and Bilee and Flu-on than he had thought. The idea interested him.

At a signal from the Head, everyone began to move

toward the amphitheater, each in his or her own way. Some rolled, some were propelled by jets of air, some walked as he did. Those who could only move by thought projection, naturally arrived first.

Ganser, Flu-on, and Bilee took their time. Ganser was still thoughtful.

"I was wrong, Bilee," he muttered, letting his mind run on. "They're not blotters. They were once like us, or at least their ancestors were. But their worlds are so crowded, they've had to make their lives a mental contest just to coninue to exist as individuals, or at least as intelligent individuals. I wonder if they can ever be different."

Bilee and Flu-on looked at him curiously. He was a little amazed himself. Why hadn't he realized that before!

"Why?" asked Flu-on. "Why is it that way? It wouldn't have to be. And I think even the ones who move out to new planets stay the same. Maybe they're what happens to minded species—and we on our planets just haven't evolved that far."

"Then I don't want to evolve," said Bilee. "There has to be something more."

"Yes," said Ganser. "There does have to be something more. Because that's a dead end. But what else can happen?"

A teacher appeared at the door ahead.

"No place for chatter," the teacher murmured at them.

The three had to separate. There were no places together. Ganser made his way to the first spot he saw, quietly, his head down, his mind still wrestling with the questions he had raised. He hardly noticed the

Head come in with a lot of others following. They had all mounted to the low stage at the front before he saw them. His mother was there! She was on the Central Committee of the Outer Galactic Council this year, but what did her presence mean? He counted the people on the stage. The whole Central Committee and the Central Convener must be there. The feeling of anxiety around him was stronger than ever, and strangely it seemed to be shared by those on the platform.

The Head stepped forward and began to speak.

"I will be brief. You see before you the entire Central Committee of the Outer Galactic Council and its Convener. They bring a perplexing problem that faces them; they come to enlist your help. I will not explain further, but will leave it to the Council Convener, who will speak to you now."

The Convener gave a long speech. Ganser felt it could all have been said more directly and in one quarter the time. But reflecting again on his new-found evaluation of the others at the school, he decided maybe the Convener knew what he was doing. Abstract ideas came quickly to his classmates, but not concepts of real physical change.

What it all came down to was that, as everyone knew, the outer galaxy was divided into fifty sectors. In each sector the majority of the stars and planets were known, although many had not really been explored. The fifty sectors, however, covered only the great spiral arms of the galaxy. The core, beyond a hypothetical perimeter, was still largely unknown. It was a place of gas clouds, of masses of dust, and of many strange stars. Exploration had tended to take place in safer, more ordinary areas. Besides, no one had believed that life of any recognizable sort could exist at the galactic center. But in recent years scientists and the Outer Galactic Council had not been so sure earlier conclusions were correct. There were signs of strange, unnatural movements in the core. Odd things had happened in the fringe areas of sectors surrounding the core. It was possible that danger could come from the core, and come fairly soon, to all the settled planets of the outer galaxy. Travel in most parts of the galaxy had been limited even more than usual while the situation was being studied.

"Because your training and inclinations fit you for such service, and because, quite frankly, we have no comparable group to call upon, we are transferring each of you to a separate command and observation post, on a planet near the edge of the unknown. Most of these will be on uninhabited planets, because as you well know, few planets near the core have been settled or currently have minded life that naturally evolved there. Unfortunately, it will be necessary, in order to cover a maximum area, for each of you to be stationed alone. You will be well provided for, of course, and will be expected to report any and all occurrences you see in the core area within your range of surveillance."

He went on with details, but Ganser's mind wandered. They had been well prepared for the Convener's deputation by his earlier remarks, but even so there was shock all around him. Shock and outright fear. Regardless of what their ancestors might have been, Ganser's classmates had never been alone, had never had an individual responsibility. He went back

175

to his earlier thoughts. They needed others around for
their own identification. They'd die of being alone, he
realized. Even here they were afraid of it. Most of
them had never had to realize that a challenge could
be real, not a hypothetical game, and could come to
the whole person, not just the mind. They were afraid
of the real, and afraid of those who could deal with it.
But the Convener should know that! Well, of course
he did, Ganser saw. He simply had no other choice.
There were too few he could call on for service of this
kind. Most people were too busy on their own planets
and in their own sectors to leave, even to fend off
what could be real danger. Few would be willing to
isolate themselves for the good of the galaxy, or would
even be able to appreciate what danger was, the kind
of danger the Convener saw.

The amphitheater was silent. No one spoke. The
Central Committee on the platform gazed anxiously,
eagerly, at the students. The students sat frozen. And
then, almost without thinking, Ganser moved. He
stood and began speaking. His thoughts were not
formed. The idea he began to pour out was not con-
sciously put together, yet he knew with a deep inner
excitement that it was a good idea and that he believed in it.

"Why can't someone go to the core and see what's
there?" he asked. "Has someone gone? Why just observe from the outside?"

The Convener seemed impatient. "Of course, we've
thought of that. Tried it, even. But no one who has
gone has returned. The forces are too strong for ships.
And it is too hard for an individual to place himself.

You know the dangers of transportation to wholly unknown planets, surely?"

"Yes," Ganser went on, his excitement growing. "Not ships, of course. But why must people land? Why not someone, or maybe even two or three, with proper suits, after some experimenting and working together, going to the space between? Looking around. There's no need to stay long. Ten or twelve places, even a hundred, could be approached in a few days' time. And then maybe you'd know. With a proper set of True Relations, and whatever other information you do have, I think it could be done. Surely some information is available."

"My dear boy, don't be preposterous. In the first place, who would volunteer for such a mission? And we certainly can't force anyone to go. It would be murder. But even beyond that, you must surely know, if you are bright enough to be here, that even those most capable of self-transportation require a specific destination and a positive landing site. A True Relation is hardly enough. No, our plan is the only solution for the present."

Ganser saw his mother frown and nod her head. But he had no intention of letting go.

"I would volunteer," he said, and saw his mother look both shocked and horrified. "And I'm fairly certain Flu-on and Bilee would too."

They both stood up and nodded yes.

"And," Ganser went on, quickly before the Convener could object again, "if you'll give us permission and gear, I think we might find a way to pinpoint ourselves in space." He began then to put as much authority as he could into technical details, drawing on all he'd learned at the school, but more on what he'd learned from Uncle Britter. Until now, he hadn't realized how much his uncle had taught him.

The Convener began to look less gruff. He listened more and more intently. "Yes, yes, go on," he said at one point.

When Ganser finished, there was another moment of silence.

"You speak well, boy," the Convener said. "It's not that we haven't thought of many of these things. It's just that you seem to have had some travel experiences no one else has had. I'm inclined to think your ideas may be worth further consideration, if they are indeed based in knowledge and experience. What is your name, and where are you from?"

Before he could reply, his mother spoke. "Will you let a boy change the course the entire Central Committee has set?"

"When a boy seems to speak wisdom, yes," said the Convener. "What is your name? And where are you from?" he asked again.

"Ganser Wekot," he said firmly. "From Sector 5, Earth."

The Convener started, then looked at his mother.

"Council Leader Wekot," he said, "you have a son worthy of you."

His mother nodded weakly.

"This assembly is dismissed. Will the three volunteers come with us? We may decide to follow the plan previously set. But I feel we must at least discuss Ganser's plan, since he speaks with such confidence. You will be kept informed."

There was a small meeting room behind the stage.

The Central Committee members, Ganser, Bilee, and Flu-on filed in and settled around a raised platform. It was very like a classroom, a place made for discussion.

The Convener rapped for silence and began at once.

"You seem to have a wide knowledge of transportation, Ganser, more than I would have thought possible for one your age," he said.

"I grew up on Earth, sir. Sometimes with my mother and father, and sometimes with my uncle and aunt. My uncle teaches theory of transportation and has done some experimenting. He sometimes took me." He glanced at his mother quickly, remembering that she had seldom approved of those trips. Her face was now impassive. "He could get permission. And we never went for long. But we went to some really odd places, and we often tried new ways of getting there. Even though people on Earth like it at home, some of us like wildness and uncertainty too. And you sure get that when you travel with Uncle Britter." He grinned in spite of himself. "Anyway, I've always been interested in transportation, and I've read all I can—even here, especially here. You have to do something that takes you away sometimes, if only in your mind."

"You find this place stifling, then, and think staying alone in an outpost somewhere might be even worse," the Convener finished, giving him a sympathetic look. "Ganser, we are all different. Each of us from every place is a little different from all others, and each planet with minded beings has made a life that is in some way different from life anywhere else. Earth has an odd history and perhaps because of that has given more than its share of the new to us all. Don't be ashamed of your feelings, or be afraid to say what you know. We respect you for what you are."

"But he's so young," his mother burst out, the first time Ganser had ever seen her lose her objectivity. "And he's my only child. We on Earth have so few children. If we've given so much, why must we give more?"

"You sent me here," Ganser said. "And it seems as if from here you never get back home, even on vacation. If I can't go to Earth, why shouldn't I do something worth doing?"

"Every good thing is worth doing, Ganser," said the Convener. "And at the end of your training here, had there been no emergency, you would surely have had a chance to go home, perhaps even to stay a while as a representative of the Outer Galactic Council. That may still happen. Is that why you volunteered? And you too, Bilee and Flu-on? To get away from here? To perhaps go home?"

Ganser went through his mind. Was that the reason? No, no it wasn't. Not all of it, at least.

"I want to go home," he said truthfully. "But that wasn't it. It was more. We'd been talking, Bilee and I, about the others—all mind and no body, they seem, a lot of them. They seem satisfied here mostly because they have others to push against, just as they do at home. They need others around all the time to give them a sense of existing at all. When you told us about the outposts, they froze up. On their planets, only minds have adventures. They'd die at an outpost alone. I'd hate it, being trapped there, unable to get around, having to spend all my time on one thing. But they couldn't function at all."

"You're at least partly right, Ganser," said another committee member. "I come from a crowded planet, as indeed most of us do. Survival would be hard at an outpost for one of us. Yet, in the Central Committee, we seemed to find no alternative. What you propose is a more venturesome plan than any of us could conceive. We called on the school because no other institution represents all of the outer galaxy, and because you are all being trained for service to the galaxy. The watchers obviously had to be made up of people who had a concern for all fifty sectors. We hoped that most of you might still be young enough and open enough to adapt to the new."

Ganser was quiet, and the Convener looked at Flu-on and Bilee.

"I thought it was something to do," Flu-on said. "I need to move; and Ganser's right about the others."

"And I'm not going to be left behind if Ganser and Flu-on go," said Bilee. "I couldn't stand it here alone. There's really nobody else. That is, no one who seems to be thinking and growing the same way we are."

The Convener was thoughtful. "I wasn't going to bring this up," he said. "But when the school was founded, those of us who dreamed of what it might be, believed that by bringing together young representatives of all the kinds of minded life we know in the outer galaxy we might develop not only a sense of galactic unity in all of them, but a new direction, a new way that minded life in a united galaxy might move. We felt this might happen in some, if not in all who came, because the school would provide a totally new situation and a new look at patterns of life everywhere. For some races, it may be too late for this to happen. I cannot say. But I have a stirring of hope that in you three there is evidence that it could happen. You have not lost the essence of what you are as individuals and as representatives of your planets, and yet there is more in you—an understanding and a daring that goes beyond.

"Ganser, your plan holds promise, if it can be made to work. You say your uncle was experimenting?"

"Yes, sir. He has some really interesting ideas. But it's hard for him to get time for testing. I've been away two years, though. And he had done some marvelous things before I left."

"My brother-in-law is slightly mad on the subject of transportation," Council Leader Wekot put in dryly. "And I suspect Ganser is right about what Britter knows. You will also find him more than eager to cooperate. But you may not always be pleased with what you get. Britter is not like anyone else."

"We all have our madnesses," the Convener observed mildly. "Gormist," he nodded to his aide, "can you tack in on Earth and bring Britter Wekot here? And until he comes, why don't we all plan to stay. I'm sure the school can accommodate us."

The Head, who was in the room, nodded and led the way to the door. "For as long as you need," he said. The others began to follow.

Ganser hesitated. He felt he couldn't face the school just yet, nor his mother. And he needed to talk to Bilee and Flu-on. They were not moving either, as unsure as he.

"Oh, you three stay with me a bit," said the Convener. "I'm sure you're tired and ready to sleep, but I need a few more words with you."

His mother frowned, hesitated near the door, then followed the others down the hall. For a moment he had an urge to follow her, to try to explain. He was torn between his need to see her and a fear that she might talk him out of the whole thing when he did, though why she should want to, he couldn't quite see.

"Stay here, Ganser," said the Convener. "There'll be plenty of time to talk to your mother. It'll be a day or two before your uncle comes."

Ganser felt relieved. The final decision had been taken from him. He turned to join the Convener and Bilee and Flu-on.

The next two days were hectic. That was the only way Ganser could describe them. He and Bilee and Flu-on did not go to classes. And when they went out walking, the Convener went with them. In fact the four of them spent a great deal of time out-of-doors. It was quieter, for one thing. Bilee's and Flu-on's parents, and their planet and sector heads, had been reached. They had all arrived and were no happier than Ganser's mother. So there was little peace inside.

For Ganser—and for Flu-on and Bilee, he was sure—the project became more and more concrete, more and more frightening—and yet more and more attractive. Nothing had ever seemed more important. And everything beyond it—if there was to be a time beyond—lost any sense of reality.

Ganser's uncle arrived on the second day, even more pleased with the project than Ganser had thought he would be. There was another conference of the Central Committee, with Ganser, Flu-on, Bilee, Britter, and a few added specialists who had been called in. Ganser had been right, his uncle did have some new techniques—some tried and some not—all of which might help.

"But if Britter is the proponent and originator of these untried ideas," said Council Leader Wekot, in a last attempt to change the direction of things, "why shouldn't he be the one to go and perhaps some other adults with him?"

"Because these young people, with their new approach to the galaxy, an approach you yourself hoped would develop, are without a doubt the best observers in this thing," said the Convener, wearily. He'd said almost the same thing to too many people too many times, Ganser thought. Why didn't they leave him alone and get on with it?

Several committee members nodded in agreement with the Convener, and there was no more debate. The issue was settled.

There was a sense of relief in knowing it was really going to happen, Ganser found. That the training for the actual travel could begin. And when the committee and the Convener left to go back to their more usual concerns, the work did begin.

"Your uncle is a slave driver!" Flu-on complained one day.

"Wouldn't you think three or four hours a day would be enough?" Bilee asked. "I'm so tired, I can't think."

"Which is just what we want to help you with," Uncle Britter said, coming up. "The probability is that you'll be gone at least a day and maybe two. Or you may decide to come and go over a longer period of time instead, making many short trips. But either way, you have to be prepared to keep going, if necessary, for long periods of time. You don't know what may happen to you. You need to be able to think for several days, not just three or four hours, no matter how tired you become. And you've got to have your technique so firmly established that you can use it even asleep."

No one of the three could argue with that.

The days were spent not only in studying theory and experimenting with travel, including trips over quite long distances, but also in studying available core charts. They also had to learn from various specialists where the key spots for observation were—those nearest seeming centers of core activity—develop the needed skills to operate the miniature observation equipment they would carry along, discover what to look for, and be fitted with special space suits that would maintain life for a minimum of two days, it was hoped, in core space.

The project became more and more the only reality. The rest of the galaxy, even life at the school—which went on all around—was generally a haze at the periphery of existence for all three of them. Ganser thought of the other students sometimes, wishing he had tried harder to understand them, to get to know them. Maybe when he came back. . . . But that was even farther beyond the haze. That was unreal.

The date and site for the first exploration were set. They were all to go to Worrly D, an uninhabited planet near the core boundary. Not a bad planet, they were told. Some stationary, unminded life, but that was all. A planet that might have been colonized if it were not so near the core. There had always been a hesitancy about getting too close, based on an unfounded but persistent fear of powerful, deadly rays from the core.

From Worrly D they would make a short jump over the hypothetical boundary to a relatively known area that had been under surveillance from a distance for a long time. If that went well, they would make farther jumps on other days to lesser known places. It had been decided that many short jumps would be better than an extended trip. It sounded reasonable.

"And when you're too tired, we'll simply hold up a while," said the specialist who was making the general arrangements as the time grew close.

"Oh, we've been trained not to get tired," said Bilee blithely. "We can go on thinking for two days, at least."

Everyone laughed and looked at Uncle Britter.

"Just don't get too big for your space suits," he said, smiling. "Or, I'll have to come and get you. And I'm too old for space rescue." It had been determined that he would go along to Worrly D to continue to coach them. Ganser's mother and father and Bilee's and Fluon's parents were to be there also. The planet site was being readied by a team and supplies from the nearest inhabited system. The three were to start from near the core not because they needed to be near for transporting themselves, but for what limited tracking of their journeys could be done.

Finally, when it was only the completion of the

camp and the tracking station on Worrly D that held them back, the three began to get impatient. You could only look forward to danger and prepare for it for so long, Ganser decided. Then something had to happen.

Finally the Convener, himself, returned and announced, "We're ready. We're going tomorrow."

The three were glad, and yet Cora C had seldom looked so good.

"How long will we be there?" asked Ganser the next day, as the group gathered for departure.

"No one knows. In part it depends on you three. And in part it depends on what you find."

Ganser nodded. That made sense. It was so obvious, in fact, he felt he should never have asked the question. Yet he went on, "And after?"

"That will be decided later on," the Convener said quietly. "First we have to begin."

There was no putting it off anymore. And a large black hole of fear opened in Ganser's mind. He wondered if the others felt the same. He supposed they did. How could they not? He looked around at Cora C. At the pleasant sky. The two years here had been all right.

"You all know the landscape and the True Relation and the exact coordinates for Worrly D?" the Convener asked. Everyone nodded. "Then let's go before we change our minds." The Convener almost grinned at them.

He knows, Ganser thought, pleased. He knows how we feel. But he can't help us. It's too late now. He bent his mind on Worrly D. One thing at a time. That was the way to keep going.

"It's always so quick," Bilee said. "Even after all we've done, I never quite get used to it. Sometimes you wish it took longer so you could be ready. . . ." she trailed off lamely. "This is nice," she added, looking around at the low building that had been thrown up for them, the rather lush vegetation that crowded around the flat area, and high rocky cliffs in the distance. "Not at all what I thought a planet so near the core would be like. I guess I expected something wild and stormy." She giggled.

"It's a quiet place," said Flu-on. "Not even a breeze. Strange no one's ever settled here, even though it is so close to the core."

"This is one of the better parts of it," said Uncle Britter, unexpectedly. "There are places as barren as you might imagine, and almost as wild, Bilee. Windier than even you might like, Flu-on."

The Convener looked surprised. "You've been here? This has been pretty much off limits for a long time."

"I did some experimental work in this area once. Some core perimeter research."

"A group?"

"Alone. It was a final school project."

"Did you make a report?"

Uncle Britter nodded.

"What happened to it?"

"School-holding, I guess. Probably no one's encountered it in years. They had to accept it, but no one really believed what I found."

"Did you go into the core?"

"No, just here on the perimeter. I found some of the things your stationary observers, had you sent them, might have gotten, though things may have changed. I was only one, of course, but a lot more mobile than your students might have been. There's life out there, all right, if that's what you want to know. People have laughed for a long time at Jalish Dozent's pink and green waves; but legends die hard. And I, for one, haven't laughed at that one for a long time." He seemed distant—dreaming—as if he longed for another time, another place. Ganser had never seen him like this. Had never heard about his search.

"Have you ever wanted to penetrate the core?" They all just stood there outside the buildings, no one making a move, as the Convener reached into Uncle Britter's knowing.

"Of course. But not anymore. You have to go young. You have to be prepared for change by the kinds of training these three have had, and you have to have a young body able to take new experiences. Yet, going there is the only way, I think, that communication can be initiated. It will cost. Exactly what I don't know. We simply have to be ready to pay." He gave the three an odd look, and Ganser felt a chill inside him, deeper than the fear he had already felt.

"Why didn't you say all this before?" the Convener asked, obviously irritated. "It might have made us think differently."

"No sense in it. You would have to put too much stock, and too little, in what I said. Your plans are good. And these three can do the job, if anyone can. I'm just glad to be here to see it. I wish it were me." He was still in his abstracted mood, and Ganser wondered what more he did know.

Was knowing something more what made Uncle Britter different? The thought struck Ganser sharply.

Uncle Britter was not like other people. He never had
been. Had his research made him different? He had
only been here on the edge. Could that have changed
him? And if so, what changes would actually going
into the core make? Ganser had been afraid he might
die or be lost in some unknown place. But the idea
that he might change, might come out a different person, had never occurred to him. Of course, as the Convener had pointed out, the school had changed him.
But this seemed different, more threatening. Could he
lose himself in the core and still come out a whole
person? Would they all three not be themselves at all?

The idea tore him apart, opened a raw fear he
wished he could have left covered. And yet with the
idea there came an unexplainable excitement, bigger
than any he had ever felt before. Had Uncle Britter
known this feeling long ago; did he feel it now? Looking at Uncle Britter, Ganser wasn't sure. The abstrac-
tion was still there; was he held by something no one
else could yet grasp?

"Well," said the Convener abruptly, obviously de-
ciding he would get little more from Uncle Britter,
"shall we go in? And will the first trip be today or
tomorrow?" He smiled at them.

Ganser looked at the others.

"Today, please," said Flu-on. "That is, if the others
want that too. I don't want to wait until tomorrow."

Bilee looked at him with obvious relief, and Ganser
nodded. Today for him too.

Two hours later they stood in their special core
suits in the departure room, where equipment stood
that was supposed to keep track of them. Although
their trip could not really be completely monitored, as

most trips in the galactic arms could be, there were devices of many kinds around for communication and emergency action. It was the suit, though, that was the real marvel. Ganser looked down at his—pockets for viewing equipment, a sturdy lightness all over that spoke of strength and of wave-and-force repulsion without being cumbersome. They could see and move with ease.

"You know the True Relation and the coordinates here." The Convener was making the last routine check.

The three nodded. They had memorized all that to the point of knowing it in a state beyond the deepest sleep.

"And you each know your coordinate point." They had each been given a destination a little apart from the other two. There were sometimes difficulties when more than one person aimed at exactly the same place at the same time. Even in core space it was as-sumed that three bodies could not occupy the same location at the same time. Ganser muttered his num-ber and tried to fix his mind on it.

"Then when I count four, go, all of you, and don't stay too long, if you can avoid it. Remember, we'll be waiting. Don't kill us with anxiety." The Convener was serious.

Here it comes, Ganser thought.

"One . . . two . . . three . . . four."

It worked, just as it had in practice. The three were within easy seeing distance of each other, and a few puffs of propulsion brought them together. They communicated by the finger signs they'd learned. It looked strange done by gloved hands, but it worked.

Bilee, Ganser had always thought, had an unfair advantage in this. But it wasn't her fault.

They hung back to back in a circle, each surveying with a scanner a different direction, each noting on an outside pad anything seen.

The main thing was the brightness of the sky. And the colors, Ganser decided, hastily mapping as best he could the area before him. They were in the heart of a planetary system, and one of the planets seemed especially beautiful, bathed in a soft blue-green light. He jerked himself up—a planet bathed in light? Some large planets did make their own heat. And some atmospheres had color. But not like this. He tapped Bilee and Flu-on and pointed. They turned and looked. Then Bilee pointed out a more distant planet, barely visible to the naked eye, but quite clear in the scanner. That planet was pink, and Flu-on had spotted one that seemed violet.

They had done the best they could, and it was enough for a first day. In fact, it took almost more energy than they had to get back to Worrly D.

"I never knew you were such a sleepyhead, Ganser," said his uncle. "And just to drop off like that without telling us a thing!"

Britter was joking, but his mother and father looked upset.

"Ganser, this can be called off," said his father.

"Flu-on and Bilee?" he asked.

"Still asleep, or maybe just waking," said his uncle. "Your maps and notes were just what we hoped to get."

"Ganser, are you sure you want to go on with this?" his mother asked.

"Of course," said Ganser, surprised at his own strength of feeling. "Nothing in the galaxy could keep me from going back."

It was true. He had never been so sure of anything in his life. The core didn't have the answers to all the questions he'd ever asked. No place did, not in this galaxy, anyway. But there were a lot of things he could find out in the core. He felt sure of that. His mother, he could see, knew it too. And his father. But they were not as happy about it as he. Had he changed already? He looked down and decided he looked like himself. Why were they worried? He didn't dare ask.

There were reports to make. The three made them in more detail than they had expected. They remembered every sight, every single moment of the trip. Though they had seen no real sign of life, the Convener was pleased. And even the six parents were impressed.

"Now can we go again," Flu-on pleaded. "There's more to know. We've got to get back there."

"Yes, of course," said the Convener, thoughtfully. "Tomorrow. Get some more sleep. You look as if you need it, all three of you. In the meantime, I'll call for more supplies and a larger crew. We may be here a while. It may take longer than we had planned. You were right, Britter, about our not really knowing," he said.

"Then tomorrow again," said Bilee eagerly.

"Tomorrow," said the Convener.

"And who knows what then," Ganser murmured. The excitement inside him was almost more than he could contain. Yet somehow he knew he shouldn't show too much of it. Though why, he couldn't be sure.

Two more trips were made, without incident—except for unexpected bits of information they brought back. No life had been seen, but that seemed logical. All was according to plan, except for what was going on inside of them. Ganser knew something was happening there. But he found no way to speak of it, not even to Flu-on and Bilee, although he saw that they also felt it. There were no words for it. The second and third trips had taken them progressively deeper into the core. With each trip they had returned more tired, slept longer, reported as fully. They had little time to talk alone together, yet Ganser knew that for the others as well as for himself, something was drawing them in, something was fighting to hold them in core space, maybe even take them to a core planet. It was the struggle to leave that tired them so.

Still, he would die, he felt, if he could never return to the core. He was frightened when he thought about it all; yet he didn't know what to do. Even the hope of Earth had left him. All that mattered was going in and then coming out. The going-in grew larger and larger; would the demand to come out always stay as strong? Would it always be strong enough? They didn't have to go. The could explain the problem of the coming-out. But that would be worse. They had to go. There was something there in the core that was so important, so attractive, the idea of not going was unendurable. It was all so strange, so different, Ganser finally gave up thinking about it.

"Are you sure you want to make this trip so soon?" the Convener asked, the parents looking on, as the three dressed for the fourth trip.

Ganser's mind had been concentrating on the physical details of getting ready.

"I have go go," he answered automatically, knowing he did.

The adults looked upset. They obviously knew more about the problem than he had realized. They could see the change. Maybe he was beginning to look different. He didn't know.

"You know your destination?" Uncle Britter said in his usual firm, quiet voice.

The three nodded.

"Come back, come back," Ganser's mother whispered. And Ganser was flooded with love for her. She looked tense and worried. His father looked upset and drawn. So did Bilee's and Flu-on's parents.

For a moment Ganser almost spoke, almost said, "Maybe we should wait." But he didn't. He couldn't.

Bilee's fists were clenched, all four of them. Flu-on's mouth was tight.

"One . . . . . . two . . . . . . three . . . . . . four. . . ." The familiar counting, and they were off.

They were in an area much like the others they had been to, but closer to the center of the core; brighter, more dust, more gas. And much nearer to a planet than they'd been, closer than they'd planned to be, Ganser thought fleetingly. He glanced around at the other planets in the system. They were smaller than those in the arms of the galaxy, he realized, and closer to the stars they circled. Probably heavy. A strong gravity. That might be what held the three of them and had brought them in so close, a physical force, not anything more powerful than that. Yet it seemed more.

Among the planets in the system around them, the one before them was the only odd-colored one, predominantly green. Unsignaled, together, and against all plans and instructions, they moved to the planet. It happened so quickly, Ganser wondered if he had willed it. Surely he had. Yet when and why?

It was bare. Lots of rocks. He grinned through his face glass at Bilee, and she grinned back. But at the same time she looked as perplexed as he felt. What were they doing here? Why had they come?

The three stood facing each other. It was a planet of dense gravity. They could feel it pulling at them, like lift-off in one of the supply rockets still used occasionally to take large quantities of materials from one planet to another. All three wondered the same thing, Ganser saw, without needing to speak. Would they be able to lift themselves off this planet? Was it a trap of some kind? Their apprehension became almost tangible.

And then there was nothing. Ganser was aware of his existence, and no more. The emptiness came on all at once and left him helpless, mindless. It was a trap then, was his last real thought, as he felt the change come. Standing, sitting, lying down, he didn't know. He was, he existed, and no more. For how long, he didn't know.

*   *   *

He moved a toe, a thought came into his mind, he brought his hands to his face glass, opened his eyes and saw his gloved hands, his space scope still held tight in one of them. Moving his hands, he gave a quick glance at his surroundings. He was in the departure room, Bilee on one side of him and Flu-on the other. They were motionless yet, or almost. Flu-on seemed to be staring at his fingers. Ganser glanced up and saw a ring of adults above them. None of them were speaking aloud, but anxiety spoke on every face.

Ganser raised his hand to his helmet, pushed at it, and Uncle Britter bent down to loosen the grippers. Of course, he couldn't hear them with the helmet on. But they hadn't been talking. Their lips hadn't moved. Yet, you didn't always have to make sounds to speak. Did you? Silly! Still a memory came into his mind. A hint of something. What was it?

"You've been gone two days," Uncle Britter was saying. "We were frantic. I even did a quick spec on your location myself, and you weren't there. Had a hard time getting back. Almost didn't make it. Then here you were like this!" He babbled on, totally unlike himself.

Relieved, Ganser thought. He's relieved, and he needs to talk. But Ganser couldn't. Not yet. He wasn't sure of the answers. He'd have to talk to Flu-on and Bilee. Together maybe they'd know what had happened.

"Not yet," he managed to murmur. "Too tired. Need to talk to Flu-on, Bilee. Got to straighten it out!" Things were flooding ino his mind now, and he sat up, caught up in a new restlessness. Flu-on and Bilee were stirring too, trying to sit up, looking at him and at each other. They had to talk.

It was impossible to sleep. And they didn't even need to be alone, as long as the others were quiet. Had there been a kind of hypnotism practiced on them by some minded creature—a hypnotism with a strong post-recovery suggestion? None of the three knew. All they knew for certain was that once the remembering began, it went on and on and they had little control over it.

There were the green waves on the rocky planet. Uncle Britter nodded at that. He had learned not to laugh at Jalish Dozent's waves, Ganser remembered. And then all the information. Some minded creatures with bodies in the core. Mostly small. But most life was waves. Easier to get around. Less confining. Easier to think, though harder to do things.

Most important seemed to be the need the core felt, or at least the core as represented by the planet they had reached, for some contact with the arms of the galaxy. Not possible before. Too much conflict, too much fear, too many differences. But now, maybe, in spite of some planets in both places still in earlier stages. Maybe ready now to help each other. Make a unit to discover and work with other units, other galaxies.

The ideas tumbled out one after the other. They were all there, though how or why no one of the three was sure.

"Do they represent the core government? Is there one? A council or something of the sort?" the Convener asked faintly.

Ganser sat blank, plumbing his mind.

"I think so," said Flu-on beside him, hesitantly. "But I'm not sure."

"The core center is at 84–283–60/251, and it's on a pink planet," said Bilee, unexpectedly.

"Yes," said Ganser, "it is."

"Can you go there?" asked the Convener.

"Yes." There was no question about it. Flooded with a heartening warmth and joy, he knew they could. Now. Right away.

"No, not now," said Uncle Britter. "After you calm down and get some sleep. And when you go, I'm going too."

The Convener started to shake his head, then changed his mind.

"I'd go too, if I could," he said. "Maybe someday I shall go. I hope so." He sounded wistful, longing.

They all felt it, Ganser realized, the drawing power of it. Perhaps because they all cared so much. And they were so close to the perimeter of the core. Was it good? That didn't seem to matter. What was important was that the core and its strangeness, its mysteries were there. No one would stop them now. No one could.

"If I get into trouble, don't stop for me," Uncle Britter cautioned.

"We won't know it," Flu-on murmured. "Not if it's like the last time. I hope it is," he added. "Or maybe better. Awake."

They were all three eager. Only Uncle Britter seemed apprehensive. Yet they all knew he would never decide not to go.

The Convener began to count. "One . . . two . . . three. . . ."

Ganser could not hold himself. At three he was gone, Bilee and Flu-on with him. They were at True Relation 84–283–60/251 at almost the same instant. Uncle Britter did not appear. They waited, expecting him. Then, they knew, just knew, he would not come. Too late for him, something seemed to say. But whether it was too late because he was no longer young, or too late because he had not come on the other trips, or too late because he had waited for "four," no one said.

Without a word, impelled by an idea, the three walked slowly forward. It was a heavy, pink-wave planet, as promised. Ahead were rocks, a huge circular formation of them. It looked natural. And yet it didn't. It was a ring of stone with an entrance at each of the four sides, all perfectly aligned. Yet the stone seemed to have erupted from the flat ground—to have grown there, if stones in the core could grow. Its roughness and its sheer size spoke of cliffs and canyons on any wind- or water-swept planet. Yet there was no wind or water that the three could see.

They walked boldly forward, as if they belonged, as if they knew what lay ahead. A fear caught at them but curiosity and the sense of needing to move on were far stronger.

The walls of the stone ring rose on either side of the entranceway above them. They walked through, dwarfed, like insects coming into a human abode. The circular space within was perfect—even—and yet the rock still seemed hewn only by whatever unthinking forces might tend the planet.

The inside was not like a trap, though the entrances were small and the sides high and tight. Ganser thought of traps and dismissed the idea. It was an open place, for all of its roundness and its walls.

They stood and waited. They looked and waited. Time had no meaning. The waiting was neither long nor short. They had no desire to leave. They stood and did not tire. It was a lovely place. A place to be alive.

"Yes, to be alive."

The three looked startled, glanced at each other. The sound came again.

"To be alive. And so you are. And so you will be. Alive in a world where your time does not exist. No, not that, perhaps. You bring your time with you. As some of us did, long ago. Yet, this is where you are to be. For longer than your own time would allow. Longer than you can account for. And Earth and Groad and Xenos D will all be here, for you. For all things can be—here, and in the deeper places."

There were no words to answer. But none were needed. Ganser believed what he had heard, and that was enough. Earth was a feeling. And that feeling was here. The wildness of the sky was here—as it was on only the best days of Earth. That wildness and wonder was inside him as never before. And perhaps the rocks and the winds were here too, for the others.

"Yes," Bilee said aloud. And he and Flu-on heard in spite of their suits. Was there atmosphere here then? But that would not explain the other voice. Was there another way of speaking—maybe another way of hearing?

"This is not our central place, an entrance rather,"

the voice went on. "But all will come in time." A pink wave formed out of the nothingness before them, grew deeper, grew smaller, almost their size. "First, however, we must plan. You are our first. The first of the new order. And it will always be so. There was another, once long ago, when some of us ventured out foolishly. That was too soon. And a few others on the periphery. And of course there are those here whose sources lay in the outside. But theirs was a different coming. Now, if time is important, and that is questionable, the moment is now for what is to be. And you are chosen."

Ganser felt confused. His mind was his own, and he remembered that this had been his idea. How then had he been chosen? He was bothered only a minute. Better not to wonder. Just listen.

The pink wave led, and they followed—through the rock ring—through the ring! And then they were in another place. And the ring was nowhere. It was a dream. Ganser was sure it was a dream.

Yet, much later he knew it was not. Hours had gone by—or among those who had no time, or no time that could be explained—was it hours? There were minded creatures in the core. Some with bodies, some only waves, as they had learned before. Not all were advanced; this they had known too. But as in the galaxy's arms, many were striving for—they didn't know what—a goal ahead. And unity within the galaxy seemed the next thing to accomplish. Yet life within the core was different. More different even than life from planet to planet in the arms. Some advanced races from the outer galaxy had come here long before. Yet not all could bridge the gap over the periphery. Not all on either side. But some could. They, the three of them, could.

"We would not have imagined three," one of the waves said. "One of three perhaps, but all . . . you are amazing."

"No, only lucky," said Flu-on.

"It is more—much more," said another wave. "It is training, learning, and a nature that accepts the new. It is we who are lucky. You are among those few who can go beyond the immediate. For that we are more than grateful."

"And together we will unite the galaxy," said a new wave that swept into the center of the open—yet clearly defined—space where they all stood.

"But we are children." Ganser was overwhelmed at the prospect laid out for them.

"You are no longer children. And will not be again. You are with us, a part of us. And though we multiply, slowly, we have no children, not as you know them. You will be listened to. You will go back. And you will be heard. Then you will come to us. And together, arms and core will be one. Come with me. There is much to be done."

Once again Ganser woke on the floor of the departure room. Flu-on on one side, Bilee on the other. All three sat up. No one was there. Strange! They stood, shook themselves, and looked. They were the same. Yet not the same. With clumsy space-glove-covered hands they helped each other unsuit. In their underclothes they were, again, the same and not the same.

"You kind of glow," said Flu-on.

"You too," said Bilee.

"To us, or to others as well?" Ganser asked.

They stepped to the door, found it open, and walked into a night. But what night?

"Three days, I think," said Flu-on.

"Yes," said Bilee. "Three days."

"Whose days? Oh, Worrly D. Yes, three here," said Ganser.

"It's different, isn't it?" said Bilee. "I didn't know a place could seem so different, without really changing. Or that we could be so different."

"We have a job," said Flu-on. "Then we've got to go. Do you think we need those suits next time?"

"No," said Ganser, sure. "It will be better without." He yearned for the moment of return. They would do their job and then go back.

The others were asleep, worn out with watching and waiting. But they woke up when the three approached. Uncle Britter had come home, spent and upset. There was no 84–283–60/251, not where he had gone. After that they had watched and waited, then slept.

None of the adults needed convincing, strangely enough, when the three said what had to be said. It was because they were different, more different by far than they had been before, they realized. The changes were greater, more obvious to others, than to themselves.

"There may be others someday," said Ganser, comforting all those who would stay behind on Worrly D when the three of them left again. He felt they sensed a deep loss—the thought that none of them might ever know what the three had learned. "We are only the first. The work has only begun. Listen."

The plans were laid, the discussions held, the communications planned, so those who could not cross the border would not need to. There could be a sharing of minds and ideas and wonders across the barriers—across the gap. The three made it all as clear as they could. But some ideas were never meant for words. It was hard. Words were so puny. Why had they never known that before? Or at least not known it so thoroughly.

"We will fill the gap," said the Convener. "There will be no gap eventually."

"No, that may not be," said Ganser. "There is a gap. We can't ignore it. It may always be there—at least a little. We have crossed the gap, we three, and we have not wholly returned, nor can we ever. It would be no good if everyone went. We must be side by side, not together, for we all have something to give, something we must not lose. They must absorb something of what we are. And we of what they are. But we must not all become wholly alike. Some of them may cross this way. The gap will slowly be bridged. But a bridge is enough. Uncle Britter, they send regrets. They said you'd understand, when you thought it through."

Uncle Britter smiled wryly and nodded. "I came too early—and too late."

The talks went on for five days. Others were called to join. The three seemed to have no need for sleep, and those that did worked with the three in relays. At the end of the five days, the three were impatient. Yet they went on to the last of what they had to do. And finally it was over. They were free to go. And by going, the chain would be drawn tight—a beginning would truly be made.

They left from the departure room, and everyone in the room smiled. It was the right thing. The chances were that the three would never return, could never return. They would never see Earth or Groad or Xenos D again; yet all three planets and much more would exist for them. They would be in the core, where there was work to do, and things to know, and joys to be experienced.

Where there might come the beginning of a great understanding, of a great galactic unity.

OUT FOR THE FLICKER PATH

Why am I writing this? Maybe so some sneaky archaeologist of the future can know the truth about today. Or maybe, just maybe, so I can find a sensible explanation for what we saw. After all, it couldn't have happened, could it?

And why am I plunked down in this ridiculous isolation chamber? Its technical name, the one they like us to use, is dry carrel, but it really is an isolation chamber. Well, I didn't choose it. And I've got to sit in this dirt-down hole reading this crawly book for another twenty minutes. And Chip isn't even looking at me—maybe not even speaking to me! *Your Stars Tonight!* Dut!

Don't get me wrong. I'm not really excited. Just hysterical, that's all. And I don't believe any of it. But Chip was there too. At least I think he was. And I think he thinks he saw what I think I saw. It's all very confusing.

You see, we were on our own again last night. His folks were out, and mine were busy with some drools from the Chamber Society. There was another one of those stupid brown-outs, just as we left my house. So the movies were out, even in that new all laser-beam place.

"Let's lift off to the park," Chip said.

"The park," I said. "In all this dark!"

"Sure," he said, and he grinned. "We'll really be able to see the Flicker Path tonight."

"The Flicker Path," I said. "Are you blued out? Since when have you taken up with the stars?"

He looked kind of sheepish and grinned again, and then I decided maybe he really had. And I thought I knew all about Chip. Sometimes you get surprised.

"Oh, come on," he said. "What else is there to do?"

So we went to the park. And he was right. The Flicker Path looked good. Like a solid thing, hanging there. All those stars. You don't see them much in the city. You forget how big the Flicker Path is. I liked it. They say someday there may be things that go out into space, right off beyond gravity, and from there the stars will be even clearer. I don't believe all that, though. At least I didn't last night.

We hunkered down on the ground and sort of stretched out and looked up. I could even see the Jar. It was as clear as anything, curving around the Great West Star.

"Creag," I said finally. "I never saw it like this before."

Chip was quiet. But I felt a tap on my shoulder. "Hey," I said, "we didn't come here for that. To see the Flicker Path, you said."

"I beg your pardon," said a voice. Well, sort of a voice. High and soft. I jumped. That wasn't Chip. It wasn't Chip by a whistle. "I beg your pardon," the sound said, like some soft loudspeaker.

"Chip," I said. "Chip?" I was scared.

"Yah," he said, and his voice was there too, but kind of brittle and hollow. The park isn't all that safe at night. We weren't supposed to be there.

"Please, you two," said the high voice again.

Chip and I were on our feet like a bolt, ready to run. And then we saw it. Or I guess we saw him. Actually there were two sorts of hims—or hers. But they weren't really. I don't know what they were. Big heads and not much more.

It was enough to make you shrivel.

"I think I need to go home and read a book for tomorrow," I squeaked.

Chip muttered, "What you kids think you're doing? You think it's Waste Weather Night or something?"

"Listen, you two," said another voice, a deeper one this time. Kind of heavy and *ruh! ruh! ruh!* We both stopped. It was the kind of voice you stop for. And we listened.

"We're visitors," the deep voice said. "We have no desire to be known here or to meet any other of your people. But we wanted to talk to someone at your stage of development in your galactic system."

Chip was feeling a little more tied together by then. They weren't very big, those two. Mostly head. "Don't put us on," he croaked. "Our galactic system! Huh!"

The first one, the higher voice, said, "Just tell us a few things. That's all we want. There are a few things we need to know. Your language we have absorbed through observation. But there are some things we can't discover that way. For example, what do you on this planet call this system?"

"What do you mean, this system?" I said, even dumber than I usually am.

"This galaxy?"

"The Flicker Path?" I said, sure now that these whispos had escaped from some wild place.

"The Flicker Path. That sounds right. Roughly comparable to the Milky Way, an old local term for our galaxy." He turned to the other and nodded. "Tell me," he went on, turning back to me again, "a little more about yourself. Your school. What is it like? Grammar, history, math, science? Or do you also have a little mind direction and space equation?"

I looked at those two again. If there hadn't been something in those voices, I would have called the gops for sure. I'm not all that much for gops, but sometimes they give you a feeling of confidence. Instead I found myself answering.

"Look," I said, "I don't know what you're after. And I sure don't know anything about mind direction and space equation. But if you're taking a public opinion poll on public education, I can tell you plenty." And then I really gave it to them. Dumb teachers. Stupid textbooks. Ridiculous parents. Useless subjects. And all for what? To stay on the same old treadmill, as far as I could see. Most of the other kids thought so too.

That opened Chip up, of course. He's hung up on world problems and how we ought to save people. He's fed up with the mess we've got here. That, and bullet-ball cars are his crates. Sometimes I think he's two people—the bullet-ball half and the world-problems half, with not much left over for anything else, including me.

Those two whispos listened, and sometimes they said a word or two to each other. But I got the feeling they didn't always have to say everything out loud to each other. Isn't that a funny idea? I don't really believe it. I couldn't see their ears, though.

Chip went on and on until he'd run down his whole clutch. Then, without really meaning to, we began to ask them questions, Chip and I. Sometimes the answers didn't make much sense. You can't tell me a star can have nine planets. Four is enough. And once when Chip asked them how they got to the park, they looked down and we looked down, and we felt as if we were all ten feet off the ground. Chip and I just looked at each other and then we began to sort of squirm, and suddenly we were on the ground again. I could have sworn I heard a giggle out of those two. You can't trust grown-ups, if that's what they were, even though they were so small and so sort of all head.

Well, we talked a little more. We were kind of having fun, Chip and I. It was so ridiculous, it was a crash, except for that up-in-the-air business. But then Chip said, "Now stop pulling us out. Where are you guys from? And what are you doing here?"

"Look," said the deep voice, "look up there. It's very dark tonight, thanks to your brown-out. Your usual smog even seems to have settled down. Now look. Right there, down from your Great West Star and to the left of the Jar, do you see that fuzzy speck?"

I looked hard, and all at once I saw it. Chip did too, but he wouldn't admit it.

"That's our galaxy, the one I said was once called

the Milky Way. It's about two million light-years away. You can't see our planet, of course, or even our star. But there's no need to. They're much like yours. Or once were."

"Now tell us another," said Chip. "Two million light-years. You'd have to spend that much time getting here, and you can't be anywhere near that age. Not even one million." Chip thought he had them there.

"No, we left home two years ago, and we've been exploring around here ever since," said high voice. "We . . . well . . . it's longer than that on Earth, where we come from. But not all that long. There are ways. . . ." The words stopped as if high voice thought we were too dumb to understand what he was trying to tell us.

"Never mind!" I said, using my best sarcastic tone. "We wouldn't understand, I'm sure."

"No, you wouldn't, you're right. But what I can't understand," deep voice said, "is how you can be so like us—like us as we were in time before our time really began. As we were in some of our oldest records. You're almost the same, in all kinds of ways. We have a few planets left in the system that retain some of these old ways. But very few. Some newly evolving ones, of course, that may produce something." He spoke almost to himself.

"Now that's enough!" Chip said. "If you're so far beyond us—then what should we do with all our problems? I told you what they are. Then how should we solve them? You ought to know."

"Don't be in too much of a hurry," said deep voice.

212

"There are always problems. They change. Patterns change. And sometimes things get worse, sometimes better. But no matter what happens, problems remain."

"Yah! You just don't know the answer," said Chip. "You think you know a lot, and you don't."

"We think nothing of the sort," said high voice. "We see some patterns you don't see, that's all. But patterns are surprising. They don't follow as you might expect. Learn everything and then jump to the unexpected, that's about all we can tell you."

"Yah, yah," I said, suddenly tired of the whole thing. "Listen, I have to go home. And if you guys have a place to go, maybe you'd better go there too."

"I guess you're right," said high voice, with a sigh.

And all of a sudden they weren't there. They just weren't there!

Well, Chip and I started to run then. We didn't say anything, we just ran. We ran until we fell up the steps at my place. Then we caught our breaths. And Chip left, almost right away, without saying anything. I went in and all at once it hit me. What had we done? What had happened to us? And who would ever believe us?

Today I headed, first chance I got, for the library. I wanted a book on galaxies. But I was a minute too late. Chip was there first, reaching for the only decent book in the place. We both grabbed the thing. And he yelled at me. And I yelled at him. We nearly pulled the ramming book apart. And that's when the librarian came.

"What's your problem?" she said, sweet and sour at the same time.

We both began at once. And then we both shut up. Who would believe us? We couldn't explain at all. Not to a grown-up. Maybe not even to a kid. Most kids aren't much for space.

"This is quite a technical book," the librarian said, taking it away. We both knew it. It was the only one that held any chance of helping us. "Here are some that may be of more interest to you. Why don't you each take one and come with me?"

So here I am in this dumb isolation booth, reading *Your Stars Tonight*. And there's Chip reading *Briley Sees Stars*. And what we both want to know is: Is there a galaxy called the Milky Way—or once long ago called the Milky Way? (But how would anyone know that?) Or, is there a galaxy about two million light-years away where they know a lot we don't? But then, no one here knows that either, but us. Or do other people know, and we just don't know it? It's all so confusing. And *Your Stars Tonight* is no help. At this rate I may never have any answers. And maybe I really don't want any.

It's kind of scary, either way. If they were from here . . . or somewhere else. It's not really about that Milky Way I want to know. (And by the way, isn't that a silly name for a whole galaxy? The Flicker Path is much better. Maybe we're smarter than they were.) What I want, I guess, is a book about the jumping. Learn everything and jump to the unexpected. I wish books were different like that. Sort of leaping out in whammy directions. I wonder if we really were ten feet up in the air last night, Chip and I? Do you think we could learn to do that for ourselves? Do you think those whispos will ever come back? Chip and I may go to see. We may go to the park tonight. I think maybe we have to go, even if no one ever comes again.

SOME NOTES ON SOURCES

The Turning Place

Very little is known of exactly what did happen on the day of the Clordian Sweep. Clordian records do not reveal what the deadly rays projected from several spaceships, carefully concealed, consisted of. The result, however, was a rapid disintegration of all carbon compounds, which destroyed all life, since all living things on Earth have a carbon base. Clusters of people in places untouched by the rays did live—some of them in underground complexes, others in areas where natural configurations of land blocked the rays, and still others, perhaps, in the centers of the initial field, where they were not touched. There are no known written records of the event as seen from Earth, but there is an oral tradition that carries some survivor stories.

Over the Hill

Just as some people were preserved after the Clordian Sweep, the fertility of some land remained. Actually the rays did not poison the ground. They simply killed the life in it, sterilized it, so that it became hard and unproductive. Only when bacteria, earthworms, and other organic matter had once more invaded the barren places, could they become productive. People lived on the small plots of productive land. They did not reproduce quickly, both because food was limited and because, scientists now know, certain physical changes in body chemistry limited their reproductive ability. Again, our knowledge of this period is based largely on oral tradition.

Enough

When land became more plentiful, the population did increase more quickly, mostly because people were able to live in larger communities and mating was easier. However, communities did not grow too large. A fear, perhaps left from the time of the Clordian Sweep, prevented this. In the new communities there was greater leisure, and eventually some of the more venturesome people began to investigate what were clearly remains of large towns and cities. A small group of people grew quite excited about what might be learned from these areas and banded together as the Pre-Clordian Sweep Scientific Recovery Group. They were able to produce an amazing number of technological improvements over a very short time. Velta Akhbar of this story was a real person, and she did invent the first land transportation system—a kind of hovercraft railroad. No tracks were needed, but long trains of cars were floated over varying terrains. Little is known of her life, but records do reveal the general tenor of existence at the time.

Accord

This story is based on fact. The Sorchum family were the first ambassadors from Earth to Clord and did in fact reveal the new nature of Earth people to the Clordian government, in much the way this story is told. Casselia Sorchum is a heroine still, though to most young people she is more myth than reality.

Catabilid Conquest

At the time this story represents, the people of Earth had entered one of their rare, stagnant, self-satisfied epochs. Though the underlying unity of Earth people was by this time clearly established, largely through the development of the sequestering system, which by this time had passed its period of greatest usefulness, the sense of gathering in all, and cherishing all for the breadth of understanding to be garnered, had not yet been completely understood. Therefore, those who were different stood outside. Since Earth was an inward- rather than an outward-directed planet, those who went to other planets, and even their children, were often outside the mainstream of Earth life. The twins of this story are fiction, but they represent a small group who brought needed changes to Earth. The early movements toward self-space-placement did come from other planets. There is a planet named Cheriba, which was once called Frod. And there was some research done on that planet at about the time this story is set. The Catabilids do exist, although few of the other inhabitants of the galaxy have ever seen them. Catabilids do not leave Cheriba, and Cheriba is now off limits to travelers of any sort, except in great emergencies.

Quiet and a White Bush

The true mechanics of a self-space-placement are, as far as the outer galaxy is concerned, a contribution of Earth. It developed in several areas of the planet almost simultaneously. This story is fiction, but it comes close to some of the true stories that are told of this time. Records for this period are, of course, very complete, so research into these developments is not difficult. Planets like the white planet are known, although they are not common. Few intelligent species have no capacity to move.

The Talkaround

Jalish Dozent still receives less honor than he should. His discoveries changed life throughout the galaxy. His life is well documented and there have been several significant biographical studies. But few people credit him for as much as he did.

A Central Question

The events of this story are too recent not to be known to most of the readers of this book. The story is, of course, based on what did occur. The three young people who moved into the core of the galaxy were not seen again, but they did communicate with relatives and with officials in the outer galaxy on a regular basis. With their help, the galactic government was instituted.

Out for the Flicker Path

As we reach out to our neighboring galaxies, we of course do a great deal of research that does not involve contact with individuals on specific planets. Sometimes, however, it seems necessary to check certain hypotheses by actually visiting a planet. When this is done, planets at every stage of development are reached. Earth people on these missions sometimes find themselves confronting people and situations that only a course in pre-Clordian Sweep archaeology can help them understand. This story is not based on an actual occurrence, but might certainly be true, given the information contained in some research reports.

Three Collections of Essays and Stories on Youth, Alienation, and Discovery from Laurel-Leaf Library

EDGE OF AWARENESS $1.25
edited by Ned E. Hoopes and Richard Peck
In this stimulating collection of 25 essays, statesmen, poets, anthropologists, critics, and scientists express their personal views on many subjects, from the problems of young people to the exploration of outer space.

POINT OF DEPARTURE $1.25
edited by Robert S. Gold
Adolescence is a very trying, frequently anguished, period of life. This collection of 19 modern stories registers the full range of the youthful experience—the pain, the confusion, the excitement.

WHO AM I? Essays on the Alienated $1.25
edited by Ned E. Hoopes
Twenty-seven renowned essays examine the dilemma of most youth today who are searching for a clearer picture of themselves, of their environment, of their society.

Two Novels by

COLETTE

Translated from the French by Margaret Crosland

Duo A masterfully drawn portrait of the disintegration of a seemingly happy marriage, and

Le Toutounier A story which

traces a woman's life after the demise of her marriage, as she seeks to bridge the gap that men have created between herself and her sisters.

Few writers have portrayed a woman's situation as powerfully or as precisely as Sidonie-Gabrielle Colette.

"She was a sentimentalist, perhaps, and a titillator, certainly—both out of sheer calculation; but she was also an artist. Colette had the intuition, the insight, that her successors so largely lack and that made the good novelist a good reader of souls as well." —*Saturday Review-World*

"A remarkable woman who was incapable of a badly written sentence."—*The Boston Globe*

"One reads her as one reads any other lyric poet. She was Colette, a magician."—John K. Hutchens, *Book-of-the-Month Club*

❧ A LAUREL EDITION $1.95